"From the Parthenon he acquired: 56 blocks from the frieze, 19 pedimental statues and 15 metopes, along with certain architectural members, from the monument." This is from the Melina Mercouri Foundation https://melinamercourifoundation.com/en/the-parthenon-marbles/the-time-of-removal-2/

In addition to the above, the Temple of Nike Apteros had sculptures forcibly removed, as well as a caryatid and a column from the Erechtheion, and a range of artefacts were also taken from across mainland Greece by Thomas Bruce, an apparent Earl.

THE AEGEAN SEVEN TAKE BACK THE "ELGIN" MARBLES

A Stolen Marbles Adventure

BILLY COTSIS

ISBN: 978-0-646-85263-8 (paperback)

CREDITS

Poetry Mytilinis Smyrna, note there are a total of ten verses from two poems by Lord Byron to illustrate points about him

Love scenes drafted by Ana Marcia, Brasil

Cover design Mame Gonzalez Braconi, Argentina

Proof-readers Sophie Papatheocharous, Cyprus; Shirley Kaptanos Katsoulako (and Mick), Sydney; Kim Appleby, Sydney; Christina Alexopoulos, Sydney; Aspasia Koulmandas, Lesvos

TABLE OF CONTENTS

CHARACTERS

Alcibiades is a young man born in Athens as one of the few with a long lineage from the city. He wants to become a doctor, and until then is content to be a tour guide, or is he? Named after a brilliant General who changed the course of the Peloponnesian War and was considered a traitor in Athens. Can this Alcibiades become a hero unlike his stained namesake?

Melina is a young woman from Thessaloniki. She comes to Constantinople to buy silk for fabrics and inadvertently gets mixed up in love, adventure, and business!

Solon is half Armenian and Trebizond of the Pontus. Named after the Athenian reformer who helped lay the groundwork for Athenian democracy. Just like his namesake, a principled man with a love of the Hellenes.

Little Monster/Lord Elgin, British aristocrat Thomas Bruce who bought his way up the military ranks, took advantage of his wife's money and used his Ambassador role to the Ottoman Empire to loot Greece. Did he do it to help the Greeks, or was it for ulterior motives? Can he redeem himself?

Lord Byron, on the surface a brilliant mind, entertaining person, thoughtful and considered a rebel in British aristocratic circles. Can Byron help orchestrate the return of the marbles?

Pierre, half French and Greek, a well-connected man and veteran of the Napoleonic wars. With a possible shady background, will he be a friend or foe?

Bouboulina, a heroine in every sense and a master of the sea. From Spetses and Constantinople.

Giovanni Lusieri, from Napoli, the former painter for the King of Napoli and a useful artist, ends up being a useful accomplice for the little monster.

Eleftheria, from the Greko town of Galliciano, she is a cousin of Alcibiades and also dreaming of studying abroad.

Anamarci, the Portuguese and Smyrna woman who teaches languages, a love interest of Alcibiades. Her well connected father is able to open the doors for her to help Alcibiades and friends on their odyssey.

Captain, all he had was one task, get them to London and back. What was he thinking?

Jack & Jimmy escaped political prisoners from the Ionian Islands. Will the British recapture them, or will they end up in Australia?

Mona, a Cyrene Greek Libyan who knows her way around the Mediterranean.

Michael Soutzos, a Phanariot from Constantinople and future Prince of Wallachia and part of the Filiki Eteria.

Numski, Turkish teacher who tries to stop the looting at the Acropolis.

Reverend Hunt, a Reverend involved with Bruce, who is more sinner than saint when it comes to the events of this era.

Assistant Rooney, a lookalike and personal assistant for Byron in Venice.

Joan, who provides Pierre with vital information about London.

Rainbow Warrior, in honour of the famous Kiwi ship

READ ME

The style of writing, historical 'accuracy' and why this was written.

In the past, I have written about the Greek kingdoms and entities that existed from the end of Alexander the Great to the establishment of Cyprus. There are at least 36. I wrote this in the first person. That first person was the foremost historian, *Thucydides,* who was suddenly *brought to life by Apollo,* to provide a unique point of view on history as the person on the ground.

Then I wrote a historical fiction novel set in Constantinople, 1453 and I created a few characters to complement the existing individuals who fought at the siege. The intent was to bring to you an overview of what happened, how it happened, why and who and who was involved? I took creative license to provide an alternative ending. Who doesn't like a happy ending? If you had read that book, you would have noticed the drama interspersed with dry humour, the politics of the day and history.

With that in mind, I replicated the formula here for the Aegean Seven.

Many of the characters in the book existed; Thomas Bruce (7th Earl of Elgin) who is the big thief and Earl, the brilliant Byron, Bouboulina, Giovanni Lusieri, Reverend Hunt, (these last two both worked for Bruce) and a few historical figures that receive some airtime i.e., members of the Filiki Eteria.

The Aegean Seven is entirely made up, with the exception of Byron. Each character represents a part of the Greek world, a world that I want you to learn about if you are not already acquainted with it. For example, Eleftheria comes from Galliciano in Calabria with an additional Alexandria heritage, Solon is Armenian and

Greek from Trebizond. Some of the characters have also featured in my short film projects in the past, notably Alcibiades and Melina. Yes, she is named after Melina Mercouri who fought tooth and nail to regain the stolen pieces from Britain.

If you picked up this book in order to use it as an accurate guide to history and what happened between 1801 – 1817, please stop now! This is and remains a historical fiction, with creative license. I do attempt to keep to a general timeline of the period Bruce was in Constantinople, Athens and Paris, and the years of removal and eventual purchase by the British Government. I try to keep the appearance of Byron in Europe, and other key moments in European history of the era, as close as possible to any real-life dates or events. My poking fun of Bruce as a little monster in his childhood, is very likely untrue. It is designed to highlight his real-life character flaws, and I make zero apology about that.

This is not meant to be a political statement novel and it is certainly not endorsed by any Marbles Restoration Committee. There are a number of action committees who do some amazing work to lobby for their return. I have deliberately not sought them out as I am not looking for endorsement or to rock any boats. They are the leaders in their respective campaigns, I am merely someone who admires their hard work. They are experts, I am not. Please find ways to support them in any way you can.

Why did I write this, you may or may not ask? It goes back to 2012 while I was living in London, and I was preparing for a return to Sydney. My mates Alex, Basil and Mitsos Seli thought they should take me to the British Museum. I had never wanted to go as I would have caused a public scene because the artefacts are being held against their will. We finally arrived by black cab I think, just a few metres from the entry when Alex mentioned that there is a Greek restaurant nearby. A much better idea; eat, drink, and leave my potential protest idle. I had a few great years in London and did not want to leave bitter, by causing a commotion.

My name for a while on Facebook, after I arrived home, was

Vasilieos Bring Back the Marbles OuzoEkato Dundee. Until a Greek woman, surprisingly, reported the name and the Facebook police ultimately forced me to change it, much to my behest.

One day in Sydney, a few of us had just finished a short film shoot called Draconian Decision of the German Drachma and we started playing around with ideas for a comedy short film. We settled on a film idea whereby a 'group' would take Thomas Bruce's personal 'marbles.' A revenge story as such! We laughed all night until tears were flowing from our faces, at what the film could be about. The short film never materialised, instead I wrote this as a compromise. Thanks though to Stretch, Maroulis, Diane, Andrew and anyone I forgot.

There are no two ways about it, the Marbles were stolen. The Earl demonstrated time and time again that he is a low life and his accomplices, a famous painter from Napoli, a Reverend and Bruce's wealthy wife were of the same persona. In fact, his Reverend also dabbled in 'stealing' and Bruce was caught out stealing a few years later in the Tweddell affair, which I cover in the book.

For lovers of the poetry of Byron, I do not assume to know what he was truly like, save for the fact that he had a massive love for the Greeks, he must have been a Greek in his past life. I mean no offence in drawing him into the Aegean Seven, the 'group'. Byron, who donated significant sums to the revolution, was eventually part of the Filiki Eteria and died in Greece, a true hero, and Hellene. He was just one of many non-Greeks who supported the Greek cause.

As for the theft from Bruce, the damage he did was beyond words. The firman he apparently had from the Ottomans was not even a real firman. He actually *did have* permission to make copies and sketches, this of course would not be denied to a British Aristocrat and the Ambassador. Anything more than that is make believe and the fact that the British Museum, 200 years later, still clings to a lie in a nation where there is a rule of law, is disappointing. The Ottomans have no record of a firman that allows Bruce carte blanche on the Acropolis, a 'firman' which in reality did not even use correct terms and did not give explicit permission to *rape* the Acropolis. The copy, which his Reverend held, was actually in Italian, not Arabic, Turkish, Greek, Swahili or Klingon. In other words, they had a fake copy or in real terms, it was bullshit. The weak defence provided by his Reverend, a certain Hunt, that they sought to prevent the Turks from damaging the Acropolis, holds no grounds. The Greek revolution came shortly after; the Turks were not (generally) interested in damaging temples or ruins. Almost every Sultan had respect for such monuments in conquered lands, making them 'personal property.' Otherwise, Greece would have been a complete wasteland in all the years of occupation. In fact, before 1900, there was far less damage done to Greek ruins, sites, and churches than the Crusaders, Latins, Franks, Bulgars, the Greek Byzantine civil wars and Normans had inflicted on Greek lands.

In the real events of this heist on the Acropolis, Hunt had a much bigger role and may have been the one who inadvertently opened the possibility for Bruce to go 'shopping.' Hunt is spared in my tale and is reduced to a periphery character, for it was Bruce and Lusieri who were more at fault, in my opinion. Nonetheless, all three men were cursed. The painter Lusieri died in 1821, under mysterious circumstances and his paintings mostly lost in a ship-wreck. Elgin, as you will see had significant bad luck with imprisonment, a cheating wife, bankruptcy, and another scandal which involved theft. The Reverend was never properly remunerated for his years of work, and last I heard, he may have attained a passage to Hell for his lies.

Bruce also gets more attention because even after all the work was stolen, he did not demonstrate that he cared for the treasures. For years they remained in crates or at the bottom of the sea. Mould, ill care and no love damaged the works even further.

Earlier, I alluded to various committees that undertake fine work trying to seek justice for the stolen marbles. I challenge you to get out there and support them; there are over twenty worldwide. Nations like Greece deserve better. Stolen artefacts, irrespective of their origin, must be returned to places of origin. Before Brexit, the leader of the British Labour Party, Jeremy Corbyn, had fallen in line with public opinion of 'commoners' and was open to returning the marbles. He is no longer Labour leader and there is no will from British Government to pressure the British Museum to return the marbles.

I put forth a challenge for you. The book opens the door to the chaotic period of Europe in the lead up to 1821. Explore this era, learn as much as you can. I also hope you can learn about all the Greek places I mentioned, from Alexandria and the Cyrene to Constanta and Mariopoulis and more. Greece is everywhere and the history deserves to be preserved, just like the sacred stolen Marbles deserve preservation in Athens, their home.

PREFACE

It should come as no surprise to anyone that a man from 'Elgin,' Scotland, could steal from the Acropolis. For, it is truly in the blood of some of the inbred aristocracy of an apparent upper class. You see, in 1568, some of these inbred folks stripped lead out of the roof of its most serene, Elgin Cathedral.

"We will pay for a number of the local rulers' soldiers by selling the lead to the Dutch," proclaimed the Scottish Privy Council.

"Great idea," said some more inbred fools, and the lead was stripped out and then busily stacked by the poor, overworked working class lads in a ship at Aberdeen. A cold place at the best of times, with plenty of fog to challenge any navigator. We cannot be sure if any of the inbred fatties were on board, but it promptly sank shortly after leaving Scotland for Holland. It never made it to any 'land.' Maybe it was the weight of the inbreds, maybe it was the lead itself! Who knows?

Back in Elgin, without the lead to help weatherproof the cathedral, the building deteriorated within decades and by 1637, the rafters had apparently collapsed. In 1640, a chap of royal pedigree and some other inbred geniuses removed more chunks from the cathedral. If only BBC existed to blast these buffoons for their ill-advised behaviour. Do you see the pattern of behaviour? Find a beautiful and sacred building and proceed to damage and dismantle parts that you desire.

The Seventh Earl of Elgin, well, you see, he had this inherent stupidity running through his veins. However, we will come back to this little fatty shortly and add to that short in stature.

First, I want to take you to a time of heroes, a true Lord that makes the name shine, women quiver and men stumble.

Maid of Athens, ere we part,
Give, oh, give me back my heart!

Hear my vow before I go,
Ζωή μου, σᾶς ἀγαπῶ.

From a seventh Earl, we find ourselves with a *sixth Lord,* one who was actually born in London, though raised in Aberdeenshire, Scotland. Same vicinity where the ship with lead sank to the bottom of the ocean. He lived for a while in the aptly titled, 'Queen Street.'

Our dear Lord, was born George Gordon Byron, inheriting the title of 'Lord' upon the death of a great-uncle in 1798. Seven years later, our Lord had published his poetry collection, 'Fugitive Pieces.'

It was around this time he met his first Hellenes. Teresa Makri, a young girl, and her mother Tarsia, as well as another daughter, Kattinka, staying at their lodgings briefly before he would embark on a trip to Constantinople. He would meet the family again in the Morea (Peloponnese) in 1810. Unlike the cheapskate Earl of Elgin, who never seemed to pay for anything, Byron offered to buy the girl for 500 pounds. An offer that was promptly refused! Thankfully.

You can see by now that Byron was developing a love of Greeks and when he moved to Italy in 1816, he spent time in cities such as Venice where there was a strong and influential Greek speaking community, as well as Armenian – he even created the *English Armenian Dictionary*. In the preface of the dictionary, Byron explains Armenian oppression by the Ottomans and their need for liberation. He made a good number of friends in the Armenian section of Venice….

Byron landed in Kefalonia, in the Republic of the Ionian Islands in 1823 where he helped pay for the Greek fleet; by December he went to Missolonghi, Morea. He brought with him 20,000 pounds, an international spotlight on the Greek revolution and a willingness to lead men into battle. Above all, he brought his big *Greek* heart, something he left in Greece when he died of illness. It is truly a Greek tragedy that the other Scotsman from 'Elgin,' was unable to die in Greece, instead he tried to kill an Acropolis that did not need any killing.

1

1770S AND A LITTLE MONSTER

To UNDERSTAND A WEE BIT about the Earl, one must return to his childhood. What makes a man become a monster, a liar, and a thief, all the while pretending to be an aristocrat from a Scottish nation known for its benign people? In fact, Grant the Scot had fought valiantly in 1453 to help repel the Ottomans from Constantinople. Byron, a Scot by the heritage of his mum and part of his childhood showed what a real Scotsman can do, with or without the kilt.

The Earl of Elgin was a young boy devoid of any pearls of wisdom. The 1770s in Elgin was a time of continued rotting of the lead-free cathedral and a time when the young boy himself was rotten. Lord Byron would eventually write a poem about him in March 1811, "The Curse of Minerva." For the Earl certainly became a curse, a name that remains cursed to this day.

Anyway, I digress somewhat. This little monster, no, he was not a descendant from the Loch Ness, for the Loch Ness at least had culture. This little monster was probably roughed up a bit too much as a fatty kid, eating too much porridge and haggis; he probably hated the kilt he was forced to wear on cold days. Unlike Greek men who wore stockings and had hair on their legs, his own bald legs would freeze. That bitterness towards the kilt ensured he hated the Greek fustanella and likely added to his antipathy towards the Greeks.

The little monster found his fellow humans would bully him

too. The egg shape of his face, with a pasty colour, potentially missing a heart may have made him appear less like a boy and more like a monster or elephant man/boy.

One day, the little monster was playing with some piglets. It was minus nine degrees, a good day for places like Elgin and Aberdeen. He was wearing his kilt. The piglets could sense that this little monster could be destructive, and they cornered him in the mud. As he cried for help over and over again, the piggies went to town on him. Filthy, bruised, and embarrassed, he eventually slipped out of the mud when the piggies grew tired and had devoured the taste of his body. The little monster in his kilt vowed never to be cornered again.

He should have known that by not feeding the piglets, greedily eating their dinner instead, the piglets would try to eat him. The kilt proved no barrier to the snorting and slobbering little piglets.

The Earl of Elgin also lived about 185 miles from Elgin. Misleading to any common person pertaining to where the Earl was from. Then again, misleading was something he would become adept at. Not possessing a sharp mind meant that the little monster could never quite work out why he gained such a title whilst living elsewhere. Indeed, these titles that included geography were somewhat of a misnomer and misleading as one tended to live far from where the title originated from. Possibly due to generations of moving away as well as titles being inherited by unworthy chaps such as the little monster.

It's probable that the little monster soon learnt that deception is a useful tool. Have an inherited title, but do not live in the region. That is a wee bit deceptive. Be a Scotsman but not wear a kilt. That is deceiving Scotland! So, you see another pattern emerging. The Earl was learning that deception was a useful tool and one that would serve him later in life.

For all intents and purposes, the Earl had a life that is to pity. The boy barely had friends, played by himself mostly and was attacked by pigs. The boy was too scared of his kilt to wear it around like a Sir Alex. He eventually became a man, only for his wife to take his manhood as she cheated on him with a better lover. Was it life's humiliations that led the Elgin to embrace art as he could admire the beauty of an artwork, hold it captive and be content knowing that it wouldn't talk back to him? Art would certainly never cheat on him.

It's this type of pity that may make you hesitate in casting the Earl as a villain. Believe, your pity will soon fade. Byron highlighted the lack of honour by the Earl, when he wrote the Curse of Minerva, to highlight his anger.

<hr />

"Mortal!"—'twas thus she spake—"that blush of shame
Proclaims thee Briton, once a noble name;
First of the mighty, foremost of the free,
Now honoured *less* by all, and *least* by me…..

'Scaped from the ravage of the Turk and Goth,
Thy country sends a spoiler worse than both.

2

CONSTANTINOPLE AND CHANCE ENCOUNTERS

FROM THE COLD AND DENSELY populated Aberdeen, where darkness can take hold for more hours of the day than one can care for, our little monster made his way to the warm, cultured and well-lit bustling city that straddled the edge of Europe – a far cry from the other side of Europe.

Constantinople is one of the greatest of all time, and it captivated the little monster more than his native Scotland. This is a city that has existed for thousands of years and has been the scene of many of history's most significant moments. The home of one of the greatest empires in history, the home of two world religions, a city of two continents and two seas.

Founded by the Greeks of Megara in 657 BC and named for Byzas, Byzantium as it was known, became an important trading colony and link between the city-states and kingdoms of Greece and the new settlements in the Black Sea.

In 324 AD, Roman Emperor Constantine made the momentous decision of renaming the city after himself and moving the empire's capital to "Constantinople." Over the next few decades, the city grew in importance, and as the Roman Empire crumbled with Rome itself being overrun by barbarians, Constantinople soon became the capital of what was to be known as the Byzantine Empire, the Greek speaking empire of the medieval times.

The Empire at its peak held almost the entire Mediterranean, Persia, most of the Black Sea and the Balkans. The peak came through conquests in the sixth century and again in the eleventh century, by which time the empire ruled over what was called the Greek speaking world, places that included Magna Graecia, Asia Minor and Constantinople.

In 1453, the world witnessed one of the greatest and most heroic sieges. The superior military machine of the Ottoman Empire took aim at one of the last independent cities of the Byzantine Empire. One of the defenders was the gallant engineer, Grant the Scot, a man of dignity and honour that no title could ever match. It is often said that when the great canons of the Ottomans' Hungarian engineer, Orban, began blasting the city's great walls on 6 April, it was the end of the Middle Ages and the beginning of modern times. With these times came the turban of the Sultan, who ruled his empire from Constantinople.

The city is full of rich cultural, religious, artistic and literary achievements. Naturally beguiling for someone with a small brain and an inbred mentality.

For the Sultan, Constantinople was a fulfilment of a Muslim prophecy and the ultimate prize for his growing empire. In 1801, Constantinople was the fulfilment of uncouth and uncultured behaviour by an apparent Earl.

1801, Constantinople

"Morning madam, I am the Earl of Elgin." A pale white, sweaty hand was outstretched.

The woman, a Muslim, ignored his hand. Motioning to the stairs.

Elgin nodded and dipped his oversized white hat in her direction as a matter of courtesy, after all he was a gentleman!!! In the background, he could hear a Mullah's call to prayer going up against church bells on an early summer's day. He was in the Fanar district, close to the edge of the Fanar district which housed tens of thousands of Greeks to be exact. It was a place where the Sultan had a ready and reliable population of educated Greek men who kept his bureaucracy ticking over.

"No Greeks, no bureaucracy" was how his Grand Vizier would put it when interviewed in a recent edition of the Hurriyet newspaper.

The pale little monster sweated some more. The heat. Sweat marks could be seen around his small groin area and buttocks. The man was not used to undertaking much in the realm of physical exertion. Was that a reason why his wife was cheating on him? This inability to undertake many physical tasks would have a significant impact on the history of Athens. For now, though, his aim was to meet a Turkish speaking Ottoman.

He finally reached the first floor. Breathing and panting heavily as if Athena herself had slapped him around. He knocked on a wooden door.

"Girin lutfen. Enter, please...."

———◆———

Outside, a Greek woman could make out the distant Bosporus. Some scattered walls, she was told they were the Theodosian walls which were built to keep invaders out.

"Good job keeping them out." She motioned with her eyes, not daring to speak her thoughts aloud or motion with her hands.

The sound of church bells and a Mullah's call to prayer could be heard. She smiled.

"Almost like my beautiful Thessaloniki, only we also have a few more Synagogues to add to the equation," this time spilling her thoughts out loud.

"Kalimera," came one man who heard what she had said in Katharevousa Greek.

Embarrassed, she blushed a little and looked down.

The man spoke to the lady in Greek.

"It is a beautiful city, isn't it?

She nodded.

"Here, us Armenians, Greeks, Assyrians, Serbs, Bulgars we all feel connected. We have no beef with the Turk on this day. We live in a city that once spilled blood. Now, we live together. Christians, Muslims and some Jews – Humanity. Imagine if this lasts forever. God will be delighted. We will be enlightened." He laughed.

She laughed at his attire in return. The man was wearing a mintan, waist coat, and loose salvar baggy trousers. A poorer man would be wearing a yelek vest, which he would normally wear for a walk.

"My name is Solon. My pappou was Greek, hence I was given a name that reflects the wisdom of a great reformer of Athens. I have been in love with Athens all of my 22 years. Even though I was born in Trebizond."

"Mr Solon, it is nice meeting you here, but I am not in the City to meet strange Armenians with Greek names from a city they have never been to. I have come to purchase fabric. I have been travelling from Thessaloniki, all night."

Solon chuckled and explained,

"My dear, I study fashion at the university. My uncle deals with fabric from the Orient. He has his offices in the building behind you."

He motioned to the building in a cobble-stoned street.

A sign explained, "Finest silk in Constantinople."

She smiled. Hesitated as she looked into his innocent brown eyes with her own brown eyes, poking through a dark black fringe from long flowing hair.

There was something innocent about the student. She could tell by reading his eyes.

"Ok, take me to your uncle, oh Solon the wannabe Athenian yet Armenian from Trebizond!"

———◆———

Solon climbed the first floor with the girl. He gave a discerning look at a shabby Turkish man who was talking to a sweaty man.

"This floor is where people come to make copies, translate and sometimes to attain forgeries. Next floor is completely different. It is a real fashion house." He whispered to the mystery woman from Thessaloniki, leaving the sweaty man in their distant rear.

They climbed to the second floor. The girl was mesmerised as wall-to-wall fabrics emerged into view.

———◆———

3

A TOUR GUIDE IN ATHENS

"ATHENS. SMALL, EASY TO GET around and with a glorious building standing at its high point, almost 160 metres above sea level." Alcibiades told his small tour group of diplomats.

"Zeus' daughter gave her name to the city. She is a Goddess of war and wisdom – something the Venetians lacked when they fought a battle on our beautiful and sacred Acropolis."

The group shook their heads in disgust, including a Syrian-Greek man who had no love of foreign occupiers.

The tour guide continued. "Athens has been inhabited since a thousand years before Christ. It took us many centuries, but we figured out democracy thanks to Solon, Cleisthenes, and Pericles. The latter only ever lost one election!"

The American consular official who had joined the session, smiled at the thought of democracy. Perhaps imagining that America would one day bring democracy to Baghdad and other exotic locations currently under colonial empires.

"On any given street you can feel it. The sense of history is here. You cannot believe how many times Athens has been at war. From the Ottomans to the Persians, we are a sought-after city.

"You mean town, my dear friend," came a voice from the group.

Alcibiades acknowledged. "Today, we are a small city. One day we will be the capital of a free Hellas, for no city in the world can overcome adversity the way she does. Beaten by Sparta, she rose again. Beaten by Thebes, she rose again. Beaten by Philip II, she rose again. Beaten by the Romans, she rose again. She will always have a spirit that can never be beaten. She is a masterpiece, she genuinely is. Every street will fill your desire to be happy. It does not matter if you are in any of my old spots of Keramikos or Pangrati or along the coastline. Let me hasten to add something else that will surprise you. Athens has some of the best beaches you can imagine. The coast all the way up to Sounio and the Temple of Poseidon, is amazing. At almost every turn you will see ancient temples, Greek Orthodox churches and potential for a future. We just need to say au revoir to the Sultan."

The group laughed, not taking the young man seriously. And who would? Clean shaven, dressed in the latest Parisian fashion he acquired from a study trip at the University of Paris.

Alcibiades, named after an Athenian General whose treachery tilted the Peloponnesian War in favour of the Spartans, seemed to want to make up for his namesake's negative role in history. That thirst meant that he wanted to free Athens. He was one of just seven thousand residents living under or in view of the Acropolis.

As Alcibiades explained to the group,

"In 1687, Venetians besieged the Acropolis resulting in uncultured barbarians of the Sultan taking apart the Athena Nike Temple to help stem the attacks by the Venetians. On 26 September, one such attack resulted in an explosion that severely damaged the Parthenon. Until the early months of 1688, enemies of both sides proved to be on the same page as they each took turns in looting the Acropolis. The Sultan considered this to be his property, yet all and sundry appeared to be deaf. There is nothing that can be done to cure the hard of hearing."

A tear rolled down his olive cheek. "That is all for today my friends. 'Malakies,'" he muttered under his breath.

A man stepped forward, chuckling.

"Big malakies."

"You heard that?" An embarrassed Alcibiades asked.

"Brother, it's ok. I have a feeling you and I have a few things in common. I have a plan, with some friends, to help our people. It is a long road ahead. My aim is to form an association called, Ellinoglosso Xenodocheio. We aim to educate people everywhere about our struggle.

"Who are you?" Alcibiades tried to ask the well-dressed man in the double-breasted grey frock overcoat, holding a purple cane or umbrella and wearing a matching grey hat.

"My name is not important. My associates will find you when the time is right. What you need to know is that we have Greek friends and Philhellenes everywhere. Past the Danube there are Greek ruling princes, Odessa which will one day be our headquarters, Paris, Saranda in Epirus, Moscow and Constantinople. The Greek heart knows no bounds."

Alcibiades furrowed his eyebrows. He was intrigued by the man with a clipped moustache and what appeared to be black low-cut shoes from Milano. The man nodded and turned.

———◆———

4

THE SWEAT FROM A LITTLE MONSTER AND A NEW COUPLE

THE SWEATY SLIGHTLY PALE PINK man was arguing the price of a piece of paper with another man. The man appears to not have showered for years. His long and unkept hair seemed at odds for what some termed his incredible artistry. An artistry for copying documents, forgeries, and languages.

He was after a fair price for the work the little monster had 'commissioned.'

"You promised it would cost me less than one pound."

"This was before I knew what you wanted exactly. The price went up. You do not have to live under the Sultan. I do and believe me; I am not for wanting to upset him."

"Considering your line of work…." the sweaty man stammered.

"My line of work is kept on the low brow; you are asking for something that could be controversial and has his name on a paper! 1.1 pounds or go elsewhere," he raised his voice.

Melina and Solon caught the last words as they descended the staircase. They could smell body odour and a foul temperament. A floor that was different to the one they had just visited.

Angry, the sweaty little pig relented.

"I will give you a bit more than one pound."

"Not good enough, but I will compromise, I will do it in Italian.

Today's date stamped as 1801. Then my advice is, get it out of the City."

The cheapskate little monster readily agreed, trying to hide the glee in his beady eyes.

———◆———

Melina was overjoyed at the new fabric and somewhat, shyly, her newfound friend. They walked and talked. Solon took her on a tour of the densely populated Constantinople.

The chance to explore one of the most intriguing cities in history, survey the old land foundations, visit the churches and monuments was just too good an opportunity to knock back; and that is what they did. They stood by the ruins of the Hippodrome, the Greek word for horses. It was breathtaking, just like her hair and face in the fading afternoon sun.

"This is where the blues and greens had fought for sporting and supremacy, including the brutal Nika riots in 532AD that resulted in tens of thousands of deaths. Who needs a virus or a plague when you can just kill each other? The venue was like the Colosseum, which could fit almost 50,000 spectators in its prime."

Next up, they surveyed the Blue Mosque, known to the Greeks as Hagia Sophia. She was amazed to be standing next to the famed church which became a mosque by force in 1453. She did not notice the person next to Solon who was invisible to this point.

And then out of nowhere, he made a dash and grabbed her bag full of silks.

The two chased the man down Romios street and into the side alley of Rumelia. They ran and ran as if the Olympiad of Delphi was their calling. The man ran and ran as if he was being chased by two younger people.

A Turkish speaking police officer blocked the path of the said thief, who side stepped the officer. As he did, he simultaneously threw the stolen bag at the officer to prevent a further chase. He yelled at the thief who kept running. The officer looked at the two.

"Greek couple on Rumelia, haha. I think this belongs to you." He said in broken Greek.

The two smiled, gratefully to the officer, who handed over the bag and exchanged handshakes.

"Merhaba," Solon warmly offered the man.

———◆———

Catching their breath now, with prized possessions back with the rightful owner, Solon asked,

"What do you do in Thessaloniki?"

"When I am not working, theatre. Many see this as a lowly profession," she stated. "I am in theatre. It was in the blood of my ancestors, and it enables me to gain a sense of freedom that few like me will ever gain." She straightened her back imperceptibly and with such subtlety that only a keen eye could see.

"What do you mean?" He enquired.

"This great city has seen many an empress rule. In society though, we remain with a limited voice. I feel equal to any man when I perform. Rather than be lowly, it makes us equal. More!" She explained. As women we are inferior to men and as Greek women, we are inferior to the Ottomans. It's tiring."

Solon was intrigued by the woman in front of him. Long black hair, curvaceous with luscious red lips. Suddenly, he sensed what many men had wanted when they cast eyes on her. He pushed any thoughts away and continued the conversation with the stranger.

As the young woman continued to speak, she explained that her father was a fighter and had served under rebels in the Morea during the 1770 Orlov Revolution.

"His name is Theodoros. They were unsuccessful as Russia failed to send enough support to help the locals fight," she lamented.

Solon offered in return, "you know these walls behind you, the remains, the land walls had been built by the Emperor, of that time, Theodosian during the early days of the Byzantine Empire. Maybe a sign, considering the name of your warrior father."

"I need to visit the land walls properly. Can you escort me?" she replied, looking for an excuse to spend more time with the Armenian.

As the daylight waned and cast evening shadows, the two strangers surveyed the land walls. She was impressed by the knowledge and understanding of her newfound friend. As an actress, she had absorbed the information her father had told her and recounted the facts to her friends and relatives whenever she could. It's why she was a good actress.

As an early evening moon crept into the background, standing on top of one of the great towers facing the Blachernae Palace, the two shared a kiss. And further kisses in a dark corner, away from the moonlight.

—◆—

They walked side by side to his humble house. He poured a drink that was imported from Lesvos for his guest to sip while he prepared the bath. Once it was ready, the small beautiful intelligent woman began to shed some of her clothes…. Another kiss happened, deeper and with a dash of desperation. This time she could feel the soft body, hair, and smell the scent more intensely. She also felt an urge towards taking more clothes off. Solon supressed his instincts, as he could really use a bath first.

She turned around as he stepped into the tub filled with hot water, a fluttering scintillating shadow projected by the fireplace, passed over her and the wall she was facing. She sat on a chair close by, gently rubbed his back, shoulders and chest. Once she felt the muscles were loose, the actress promptly decided to leave him alone so he could close his eyes for a few minutes.

As the water got a bit colder, he stepped out of the tub to find a clean towel and comfortable clothes over the chair; a costume worn by men from Trebizond. He took the towel but never touched the clothes. Despite the cold outside, he felt warm and the rush for completely taking her clothes off and the sight of her naked silhouette, came back stronger.

He met her halfway in the living room, both breathing heavily and the sound of their breath panting faster as they approach each other. Their marathon was just beginning.

—◆—

From the balcony, the early morning breeze of the Bosporus fluttered. A small boat was being prepared. Just a few kilometres yonder, the continent of Asia had its boundary. Known in history as Asia Minor. Melina sat on the European side, gazing.

A chubby man in a tanned, awful looking costume stepped aboard. He was carrying an envelope. He was accompanied by a darker-skinned elderly man carrying his bags. He glanced back (with a crooked smile) at the City.

She wondered why such a pale looking man was smiling and not in hospital. In her mind, he was the vilest man she had seen. He was not from Ottoman lands. "That is the man from the first floor yesterday," she pointed out to Solon, in a hushed tone.

They observed him for a while more before deciding that a new 'marathon' needed to take place!

—◆—

Anamarci had been in Athens for a few months. At almost 18 years of age, her parents from Smyrna wanted to find her a Greek husband from the land where democracy once flourished.

Smyrna was at once a beacon of hope for Hellenes and a place of caution. It was arguably the wealthiest city of the Ottoman Empire with its merchant trading, large port and a population that contained Levantines, Jews and Muslims to supplement the Greek Orthodox faithful.

Her family wanted someone who represented hope. They were a wealthy, well-educated family that saw Athens as the key to a rebirth for Hellenes. They had thought about Mytilene, where some of their ancestors had originated from, which was close to Asia Minor. Yet, it was Athens that tugged at the heart strings.

From the moment they arrived by boat to the large port of Piraeus, they had marvelled at the Acropolis and the little settlements that existed below her. Only Ephesus could compare. On any given day, looking up at the Acropolis made her appreciate the Greek heritage she was born into. They went to church and met priests hoping to help them find the man who would marry their daughter. They had a large dowry of land in Smyrna for the lucky man. Until then, the well-educated woman was set up in a studio teaching foreign languages.

The family soon discovered that a fifth of the city was non-Greek, the minority mostly spoke Turkish. No Greek man truly wanted to leave their historic Athens for an at-times grumpy Smyrniot.

For Anamarci, the mixture of a lower class of men, some wearing the fustanella, was not her idea of matchmaking. Her mood had soured from the time they arrived to stay in a double storey home in Pangrati, near the Profit Elias church. She had grown bored of the sermons. What was the point of being Christian under foreign occupation? She longed for her home by the sea.

Anamarci had spent weeks feeling frustrated. One day as she was walking alone, along the Temple Zeus, a stranger bumped into her. He was back peddling. In awe of what remained of an ancient temple, as if he had never before set eyes on such wonderment.

"Watch yourself, sir!"

"Apologies! I was just admiring the temple."

"You must be a visitor. You should just sign up for a guided tour….." she half-heartedly joked.

"Embarrassingly, I am the tour guide." He smiled, half beetroot red and not because he was Scottish, for he was a proud Greek.

He continued, "I never get tired of our history. Every day I find something new in the ruins. Look carefully, from one angle and then take a different view. You will see that many times, the static view has multiple dimensions."

Anamarci was intrigued, yet at the same time felt sorry for someone who was fixated on the ruins.

"Look sir, best be on your way. I cannot say I share the same sentiment as you. Kali senexeia."

Before he could reply, she was off again. Alcibiades started gazing again, though this time it was at the figure that was getting smaller and smaller in view.

5

AN ATHENIAN SERMON

STANDING PROUD, ALCIBIADES WAS DELIVERING a 'sermon' to interested tourists.

"Every day in Athens people stroll past ancient statues; statues that were sculpted in classical times. But imagine if these statues could talk and tell their stories; stories of a culture and a language that are far removed from our current world of printed books and newspapers. Well, somewhere in the Mediterranean, there are statues that seemingly spring to life with their stories and history! Deep in the mountains of Calabria in Italy, ancient Greek statues exist, except they are very much human, and they are the guardians of Hellenes' ancient past, a past that seemingly existed only in the history books. These human statues are the link via an oral language that has survived for over 2,800 years, surviving conquerors, disasters, population decline, religious conversions and poverty to remain one of the richest spoken tongues in history.

That language is Greko, a Greek dialect and arguably the oldest remaining Greek dialect in the world. It is a connection to the ancient Greek colonists who once spread across southern Italy. The Latins called it Greater Greece – Magna Graecia, with the name Graecia being of real significance since it was given the name Greece and has only really been used since independence, while across the Adriatic, this name from Epirus was used to describe the Hellenes who dominated the entire region from Napoli and the outskirts of Apulia to Sicily.

Sitting in the heart of the mountain at Aspromonte, exists a special town. Picturesque, it is almost as though it has been forgotten by time, with its authentic, traditional homes, narrow streets, and pathways where 600 people live. Just like Athens, the town of Galliciano is hilly. Perhaps this is Calabria's natural Acropolis, but rather than temples it is a gem of a village with its living, breathing statues. Galliciano for easy reference, is pronounced GaddiciAno (insert strong Calabrian accent here) and was established by Greeks in the 700s as Galikianon, possibly named after a prominent land-owning family. The drive up the mountain is spectacular, as though this is another Athens or Constantinople."

The crowd of foreigners nodded and gasped at the newfound revelation of a Greek peoples that are compared to statues.

"Meet my cousin, Eleftheria. She was born in Galliciano. Her mother is from the Greek and Arabic speaking city of Alexandria, now under the rule of the French. We Greeks are everywhere and nowhere; meaning we don't currently control our destiny."

"E cali emera fenete a ttoporno (a good day is judged from the morning). Thanks cousin. Hello everyone," Eleftheria spoke in a Greko dialect, "tis proti sperni, proti sianonni (who ever sows early, reaps early); I hope you have enjoyed the tour this morning and a side history about my homeland where I was born 18 years ago. We speak an older version of Greek, maybe we are like the ancient Greek statues you see here," she smiled, mischievously. "Enjoy your day and our wonderful Athens. Not all the Greeks are statues."

The crowd clapped and slowly dispersed.

The cousins laughed and smiled under the glorious sunshine.

"Now for your history lesson Eleftheria," mused Alcibiades.

She playfully rolled her eyes as her cousin rehearsed his speech about the temple, yet again!

"Over many, many years the temple of Zeus has been torn apart by occupiers and citizens alike. 104 original columns, we now have

20 standing and a few more scattered around. You can find parts that were used for houses, churches, a mosque in Monstiraki and target practice. Sixteen columns remain standing. Nothing remains of the cella or the great statue that it once housed.

Maybe the site was unlucky as it once was the site of a temple commissioned by Peisistratus, a tyrant. The building was demolished after the death of Peisistratus. The subsequent temple was drafted by a range of leading Athenian architects in the Doric style; columns were made from limestone. Aristotle once complained that the site was an example of the tyrannical excesses that had existed in Athens, though the temple was never truly finished until a half-hearted attempt by Hellenic Seleucid King, Antiochus IV Epiphanes. The King used pentelic marble, replacing lime style and switched to the Corinthian version for presentation. It was, however, the Romans who finished the temple of Zeus. At the end of the day, greedy occupiers and locals desecrated the temple."

Looking at Zeus' temple, Alcibiades explained with passion to his cousin,

"Thank God, no one has taken too many items from the Acropolis, for this would be a sin beyond comprehension," she replied.

He stood, patriotic and at full attention to marvel at the site. "Let us see what the new century brings Athens. I will always protect Athens. I want her to be free."

———◆———

The sea and winds had made the voyage rocky. The merchant ship was owned by a woman named, Laskarina.

The Greek woman made every effort to learn about her passengers. She was particularly intrigued by a rotund little monster who remained as quiet as possible. The Agamemnon* ship had picked up the Scotsman and his servant in the beautiful harbour of Mytilene. Their little schooner had blown off course and needed repairs, so it pulled into Mytilene a few days earlier.

Laskarina, sympathetic, and already filled with passengers and quality stock from Lesvos, picked up the pair at no charge.

"Where did you come from, before the beautiful city of Mytilene?"

Coldly, the pale sweaty man, who seemed seasick responded, "Constantinople."

"I was born there, though I lived mostly in Hydra and Spetses. Little islands off the Morea." She responded. Continuing,

"Are you a friend of the Ottomans? My father fought in the Orlov Revolution in the Morea. It failed…."

"I am a mere Scotsman, my lady."

"Ah do you know of the engineer, a friend of the Hellenes, Grant the Scot?"

He shook his head as the waves rocked the ship.

"He fought for our Emperor in 1453. One day, I will raise the insignia of the last Emperor of Constantinople on my ship."

The man simply looked down.

"I am not good on the sea. The sea is not my friend, I am afraid of the space, the movement and its depth." He sweated.

"Do not worry Mister, we will get you to Piraeus safe and sound." Laskarina replied sympathetically to the man.

Poseidon had one last chance to make amends for a future travesty. However, it is likely the presence of the graceful Laskarina acted as a guarantor of safety for she was a true heroine, gutsy, beautiful and admirable. There was something about her that the universe wanted to preserve, was it her beauty or her strength, maybe both.

———◆———

Alcibiades and Eleftheria made their way to the port, Piraeus. Yet again, a cloudless day had overseen the 40-minute journey by horse and cart. They were eager to receive news from Constanta, on the Black Sea coast. Alcibiades had applied for a study and work program in a city that had 29% Greek speakers. A home away from home!

He already knew that from 1802, his life would be somewhere in faraway European lands, learning and working. Probably Constanta.

As the mail boat arrived into the quiet port, another was already disembarking, disrupting the quiet facade. On any given day, it was just another vessel.

"Cousin, look, look at that beautiful woman. All dressed in a white and Aegean blue dress that shows a woman of curves and beauty; her black hair covered by a yellow embroidered silk head scarf. Wonderful fashion!" She delighted before adding, "behind her, that is one very pale ale of a man. Certainly, no Greek or Tourko."

Eleftheria was transfixed on the stranger. He was moving slowly. A gypsy tried to sell him some cloth to wipe his sweaty face. He pushed the gypsy to the ground. The gypsy stood up and yelled at him before Alcibiades intervened.

"Stranger, it's ok, he will leave you alone. Sometimes one can see a stranger and hope for business."

Turning to the gypsy in Greek,

"Let the foreigner be. Next time I might be in need some cloth, ok? Here, take this small change."

The gypsy clasped the money, shook Alcibiades' hand and was soon gone.

"Ok, I am fine young man, thank you. Say, how do I get to the Acropolis?"

"There are two of you?"

"Yes, young man."

"Well, you can take the horse and cart, a luber, that brought us to the port. The driver is a friend of mine. He will take you for free."

"That is mighty kind of you. I hope we meet again one day," the little monster was being cordial.

"I'm sure our paths will cross; the universe and God, they act in ways that not even Socrates could explain!" Alcibiades laughed. "Kalos eirthes, welcome," he added.

The sweaty man, not grasping the intended humour looked blankly.

"Thanks again," he replied, coldly.

Soon the sweaty man, who was wearing a beige hat, was on his way to the Acropolis with his man servant. The servant appeared to be a Priest, though it was hard to tell as he was kept in the background with a tight black coat that was buttoned from the neck down to the waist and he appeared to be walking behind him.

———•———

6

QUICK REWIND TO 1799, NAPOLI
A LAND OF PIZZA AND PAINTING

THE CAFES OF NAPOLI WERE buzzing. In a quiet corner of the picturesque harbour, a group of Greko speakers were enjoying a coffee and a game of cards. Birds flew low as the breeze was gentle. One would think that the Greek founded Napoli was still a vibrant Greek city if the jovial group was an indication. Sadly, Greko had stopped being spoken long before the year 1799. It just happened that the Greko taverna was a magnet for Greko speakers in the south of Italy. Some were working in Napoli and others just passing through.

Eleftheria, who was still at school, was visiting with her mum as they had to purchase materials for their school in Galliciano.

"Mama, that man seems to be staring constantly at our group."

After another round of coffee, one of the men stood up and went to speak with the staring Italian.

"Can I help you friend?"

"Er, senor, my apologies, I do not wish to disturb. I merely want to hear some Greek spoken. I am an artist.

"He looks like a Con artist…." Eleftheria whispered to her mum.

"I mean you no harm. I am being commissioned by Lord Elgin from Scotland to undertake drawings of the glorious Acropolis. I will be visiting Athens as soon as I can set sail. Most likely I will leave next week."

"This sounds like an interesting project. You may join us for a coffee. You know, if you sail from Apulia, most of the region remains a Griko speaking or Griko cultured land. Their dialect is a bit different to ours."

"Thank you, Senor, thank you. My name is Giovanni Lusieri. I am happy that you are letting me join your group. The Lord is to pay me 200 pounds annual salary, so I am happy to buy for everyone here!"

"I have a bad feeling about this man Eleftheria. Anyway, when you get to Athens in two years' time for your study, maybe keep an eye out for him!" Eleftheria's mum whispered to her.

"Can't wait to get there. My cousin Alcibiades tells me it is the prettiest place in all of Europe. Historic. It will serve my history studies well."

Mother and daughter hugged, with the beautiful port behind them.

7

1801, PRESENT DAY, WHEN BANDITS MEET AT THE ACROPOLIS

THE PERSPIRING AND NOW LIZARD looking man had made it to the Acropolis. He was met by a man with a bob cut, lighter features, and sad bleary looking eyes. He towered over the Scotsman.

"Mr Elgin, I presume," asking firstly in Italian, French and then finally in very broken English.

"Earl. Please always address me by one of my titles. I presume you are my artist."

He nodded.

"First act of business on the agenda, we need to gain entry to the site. Once in, you and your workers can survey and sketch to your heart's delight. We will also be able to remove a few stones here and there."

"Elgin Earl sir, once I understand the dimensions, I will construct scaffolding around perimeters for a better view and better way to operate….. especially if…."

The 44-year-old paused. Appearing distressed, he then looked down at the black leather Roma made shoes. "Especially if we are to take small pieces or more, as has been suggested by letter from your Holy Man." Saying out loud what he must have felt was beyond his original scope of sketching and making bust copies of the statues. He sighed.

The sweaty man looked blankly at him, perhaps not compre- hending what he really wanted to achieve at the Acropolis. Two minds under a cloudless, clear sky. Perhaps confused by what he really wanted or what his Reverend wanted. After a brief pause, he added, "let us get to work, shall we? Just let me have a word with the sentry."

Walking like a penguin, perhaps due to chaffing or from the long journey, the Earl approached the guard, seeking permission to speak to the Dizdar, the Ottoman in charge of the defence of the Acropolis.

Speaking via an interpreter, the Dizdar became animated and ushered the pale man away. It wasn't the first time he had done that to a representative of the Earl, for Lusieri had tried on previous occasions.

The Earl and his entourage decided to leave.

The next day they returned.

"Please, you must understand that these sacred sites belong to the Sultan. We cannot allow you in here. The 'Firman' you have is in Italian. I can assure you; the Sultan would not allow you in here."

Then the following day, Lusieri tried, he spoke to the Dizdar in French.

"I am the King of Napoli's personal painter. Our city was once Greek. We have a connection to this sacred site…." The Dizdar was unmoved and rigid, much the same as one of the ancient statues adorning the Parthenon.

A few more attempts were made before finally, the little mon- ster played one last card in his deck. He offered the Dizdar a salary to match that of the Sultan's pay.

"Welcome to the Acropolis Mr Elgin, have a nice day…."

From that moment on, the Earl and his depressed looking en- tourage were essentially unchallenged and unperturbed as Lusieri set up scaffolding and went about organising his men to undertake a few sketches and collect loose stones and small pieces of stone as had been the 'agreement' with the Earl.

One day, the artist was taking a mould of a sculpture. This was to create a replica when a Turkish man brought him a Tsai.

"Do you speak French?"

"A bit sir."

"Why are many of these statues missing and other sculptures missing marbles? It appears many of the statues I had expected to see are not here. Why would this be occurring?

"Efendi, many times these have been taken away and broken up into bits and pieces to be sold to foreigners who visit."

Horrified, the Neapolitan had a thought bubble inside. His lovers would often tease him that there was very little going on inside his mind. Even in the bedroom he seemed devoid of ideas and an ability to think, his brain was like a cloud blurry and hazy. Yet, as the morning sun began to fully expose itself, he had an idea. Lusieri returned to a thought that had been implanted in him previously by the Reverend from Scotland. He just needed to find the Earl.

"Your Majesty….."

"I am not a Majesty."

"I see. Semantics. It's just like me saying any sculpture here is important, even the copies, but is it?

"Your point?"

"We need to take some of these valuable items away from here, away from the heathen and to a safe destination. The Turks and maybe some of the Greeks, cannot be trusted. Your Reverend had tried to explain that to me in his letter, and I took no real notice until now. We are surrounded by heathen."

The little monster, wearing a scarf around his neck to protect him from non-existent mosquitoes continued to sweat. Soon, he would need a bucket and a rope as he appeared to be a human well, dripping in liquid from head to toe.

"What are you suggesting?" He squinted at his painter.

The painter or rather the con artist (take your pick), tensed a wee bit and cleared his throat.

"To save these precious beauties, we need to take them far from here where it is safe. We can transport them by sea. I think your Reverend will agree to that. We kidnap or rather sculpture-nap priceless artefacts, many that are attached to the temples, and we then transport them via rough seas to Scotland. We hope that no pirates, French or Irish attack the transport or that Poseidon won't make the sea journey too difficult."

"Precisely….," the Earl snapped at the painter.

"Last week my dear Lord…."

"Earl is fine," the Earl snapped again.

"Anyway Earl, Edward Clarke and John Marten Cripps, were duly granted permission to remove a statue of Demeter in Attika. Now, ask me how he did this!"

"Ok, I will bite, how?" The Earl duly bit.

Lusieri continued. "I met the governor when we had that dinner for Ottoman officials. I kept friendly relations and then I arranged a bribe from Mr Clarke, and I drew a picture for the governor to present to his wife. Now, ask if that was all."

"Come on, do tell."

The painter started again. "The governor was impressed with the bribe and the drawing, he threw in a statue of Pan, an ancient comic mask and a figure of Eros. I understand that Clarke is now loading all of these onto a boat with the aim of getting these to Cambridge."

"Fascinating. You are proposing a similar pathway. You must understand, we don't have real permission to remove important artefacts."

The Neapolitan artist laughed, "Permission?" He almost fell over laughing. "Of course, permission. "Never forget we are here to save these ancient achievements from the present-day peasants.

The Earl scratched his itchy scalp with such vigour that dandruff flakes fell to the ground. He was thinking about what the painter had told him and his curiosity was too much to bear from the look on his face.

———•———

8

FAST FORWARD 1821, WHAT BECOMES OF UNWANTED GUESTS IN ATHENS

IN ATHENS, NEWS HAS FILTERED through of the revolution, in the Morea and Wallachia, past the Danube.

Giovanni Lusieri is fast asleep in his cosy flat near the Acropolis. Comfortable in his knowledge that he had 'saved' Greek treasures by forcefully removing them from Athens, for a fee of course because acts of benevolence need to be rewarded! A sudden gush of wind envelopes his flat, strangely only his premises. None of the neighbouring premises are affected. Oddly, an outline, as if drawn or sketched out, appears in the distance. A real beauty to the eyes of the beholder.

The artist was just waking from his slumber and a night of debauchery and drinking is starting to feel a weight dragging him down. Unable to resist, unable to stand, the artist cannot fight the desire to sleep again. He chokes, he screams. A pitiful scream from someone who was tough enough to 'liberate' statues from Athens and Greece, especially Demeter and yet his scream could send a building crumbling from his foundations.

Lusieri slumps. A soul departs for Hades, for he is no more. He had complained bitterly that he spent too many years working for

Elgin and not enough finishing his own works. Upon hearing of the death, and in an effort to make this right, Elgin commissioned for almost all of his paintings to be transported to England. A noble gesture from an ignoble man.

The real Demeter once more teamed up with Poseidon to ensure that the ship carrying the works sank without a trace, in 1828, somewhere in the Mediterranean. A fitting end, perhaps.

9

PRESENT DAY, 1802, GREEK TIME AND A GREEK TRAGEDY ON THE ACROPOLIS

THE END OF JULY IS a tough time to be in Athens. 40-degree days are not uncommon. Colonial slaves were not permitted to act as human fans in places such as Athens, ensuring that rotund little monsters would struggle through the excruciating weather.

To combat the heat, the little monster had a plan….

"Ambassador, good idea to start at the crack of dawn, it's a good temperature for you and your countrymen," motioning to a rag tag group of English.

"Yes, that is a masterstroke to have scoured the taverns by Piraeus looking for crews that had lost their money to card smart Greeks! They need this job until they can pay their debts and head back out to sea again."

Five seamen and the carpenter from a British ship, looking worse for wear, had arrived in Athens. They had been hired by a certain Reverend Hunt, a man who was in business with the little monster for his soul and money. None of the crew were interested in the art or the shrines surrounding them. They looked dishevelled and grumpy, but the lure of cash can make any monkey jump. That same lure had also resulted in 20 labourers from Athens, also in need of a cash supply and the little monster was ready to turn the tap on.

One of the English seamen turned to a labourer as they entered the Acropolis.

"What is this place? Needs a lick of paint, ey?"

"The genius architect Phidias and Pericles are mostly responsible for this creation I heard from a Turkish guard. I am not Athenian, it's not for me one way or another."

With hands on hips, Lusieri, shouted at the men in Italian and French to stop gossiping and get ready to mount the Parthenon.

The sweating man, a waterfall in Athens, looked on. Deep inside he knew there was no turning back. But turning back from what? He motioned to the artist to commence.

Within an hour, scaffolding, ropes and climbing instruments were in place. All eyes were soon transfixed to the sculpture attached to the upper tier of the Parthenon, a young Greek and Centaur in battle, fighting. There was no fighting from the Greeks in Greece, just yet, only an unwanted sacrilege of a building that had not once harmed the sweaty pale man.

By siesta time, the thieves had succeeded in lowering the once securely attached marbled sculpture. It took a significant amount of care and time to attain this. Ali Baba would have been proud of this lot.

As it was lowered, all the men and a few Turkish guards nearby surveyed, proudly, their heroic deeds in defeating a static sculpture. The piece had neither attacked nor insulted them. Yes sure, the young man was not attired properly, but hey it was after all 2200 years ago when nudity was the norm and clothes sometimes in short supply.

Somewhere in an unmarked grave at the ancient Keramikos Necropolis, a small earthquake was felt at the Acropolis. Phidias was turning and shaking.

Next morning, the start of August and the countdown to the traditional holiday and festival of the Virgin Mary, when Greeks are expected to be free of sin, the men came together again. To sin.

The same ritual as the day before occurred. Usually, a ritual on the Acropolis belongs to the ancient Hellenes, who respect the sacred nature of the site. Today, there would be no respect.

The robbers had come to steal, and no one was going to stop them.

As the group once again commenced their audition for a ticketed entry to Hades, a man on a donkey rode up to the sweating pig and his (Con) artist.

Dressed in traditional Turkish attire, including a Fez and long flowing moustache, he dismounted.

In French, he raised his voice, asking the group to suspend their work immediately.

The pig asked him who he was.

"Sir, I am a teacher, Mr. Numski. I am a guest in this great city, I am from just outside Ayvali. We have a love of Greek artefacts in Ayvali, and we protect them. We may sometimes be at war with the Christians, but we have no need to damage their history and past. You sir need to stop what you are doing."

The First Mate from the crew, a big orange ogre of a man, grabbed a stick and hit the ass, not Elgin's, but that of a donkey and the donkey (probably due to surprised fright) ran away. As the teacher was remonstrating with the foreigners, the ogre king hit him from behind.

A cowardly act from someone who could barely speak his own native English, let alone French, Turkish or Greek and was unable to understand the pleas and articulated reasons that the teacher was giving.

The teacher fell to the ground. Blood streaming from his head. The ogre grabbed him again and took out his knife, pressing it against the throat of the innocent victim. "I am not a fan of teachers or minorities for that matter."

No further words in any language were needed. The teacher slowly moved along. He cursed. A Reverend who had hitherto remained in the background came up to the teacher, offering an apology and money. The teacher scorned him. "You are not a man of the cloth…." He stumbled away in disgust.

A few years later, the teacher learned that the ogre was detained by the Sultan's military for hitting an elderly woman and harassing other women. As the teeth of the ogre rotted, indicative of his kind, he too also rotted in a prison on Makronisos, never to be heard of again.

———•———

By siesta, on day two of the great Acropolis robbery, the bandits had succeeded in bringing down another precious monument. This time, cracks, small holes, and scratches were the reward to the Temple.

The men cheered as if they had beaten Alexander in the Olympic Games to claim a wreath and the honour to wrestle naked!

By early 1802, the rapists had taken at least a dozen pieces. Not stones, loose rocks or even small souvenirs. These were large pieces and with each of the parts being removed, the Acropolis bled. She wept.

———•———

Winter had been unusually cold. It had dropped snowflakes, a rarity for Athens. The great Goddess had ensured that the city would always be free of snow, yet this winter, the Goddess was also crying out loud. Not everyone was listening.

Alcibiades and his cousin Eleftheria had wondered what had made Athens snow. They had spent most of the last several months studying for their chance to learn abroad. They had engaged a teacher who was fluent in French to help them learn the language properly and to become fluent. The lessons had paid off.

"Teacher, being our last class with you, we want to ask you a question."

"It is a right of a student to be inquisitive."

The cousins smiled, and Eleftheria asked the question, "Ogretmen, respected teacher, you have a nasty scar on the back of your head. When we first met you, there was no scar."

The teacher sighed.

"What happened?

"I was jumped at the Acropolis from behind when I confronted some foreigners for taking monuments off the temple."

The cousins looked at each other in disbelief.

I tried to reason with them. I told them there was a curse waiting for them, for taking properties belonging to the ancient people of Athens. I offered them money. I tried! One sweaty man claimed he had permission from the Porte. He produced a letter. It was in Italian. From my short years in Smyrna, I learned to read and write that language. I found it hard to believe. As I was assaulted, the men said if I tried to stop them again, they would tie me to one of the boulders and throw me off the Acropolis. He took my paper ID from my pocket and explained this would happen if I ever spoke a word of the incident to anybody.

"Merhaba, teacher. Your secret is safe with us. Thank you for trying."

The three hugged. It would be the last time they would see one another in occupied Athens.

10

ANAMARCI

ALCIBIADES MADE ENQUIRIES, DAILY, TO some of the people who lived near the Acropolis. Very few people had seen anything unusual until he bumped into Anamarci.

She was an unusual woman. Tall, beautiful and was Portuguese and Dutch through her father and Greek from her mother, who was born in Tsalka, Georgia, though that lineage had come from Lesvos. Her parents had met and lived in Smyrna.

Anamarci had quietly observed the occasional coming and go-ings of English-speaking tradies from her little school where she taught geography and languages. One day, a man with crooked teeth tried, in vain, kamaki – a form of trying to impress a woman. The young teacher, using her hot-headed Portuguese streak told him to go and go fast. It was then that she came to notice the men a bit more over a period of a few months.

Every few days, they would transport materials and bags from the direction of the Acropolis. She could never tell what was in the covered carts, though she was suspicious of the men.

Alcibiades had all but given up on learning more from the people near the Acropolis when he stumbled upon the small teaching studio.

Immediately struck by her look, his olive skin soon turned to beetroot and clothes tightened. His legs trembled as he approached her.

"Excuse me, errrr, um…."

"Yes sir, how may I help you?"

"Well, um…."

"Sir, please collect your jaw off the ground. When you know what you need, please be sure to let me know. I work inside this teaching studio behind me, and class is starting soon."

Alcibiades, with the said jaw, stood motionless. A bit like a statue on a cold day in Elgin. The young woman was familiar to him.

Alcibiades walked past the studio daily for the next few days until he finally found the courage to enter the studio.

"Maam, I am sorry to bother you, I am a tour guide…."

"Yes, I know who you are. There are not too many who undertake your work here. I hear you have an unending love for our fair city. And…. You love the remains of the temple of Zeus!" She exclaimed, alluding to a previous brief encounter at the temple.

"I do, I do. And it is also part of the reason I am here now."

"Part." She smiled and laughed.

"Aside from the fact you are the most beautiful thing since the Acropolis, I need to ask if you have seen any unusual activities from the sacred site."

Without blinking at the compliment. "Indeed, there is some occasional activity involving a number of English seamen, a few locals and an Italian. I am familiar with art and painting, and I learnt just yesterday he is a man who paints for the King of Napoli. He is now working for the British Ambassador, not as a painter, rather as a thief. I am told a Reverend is helping them too. My friend, she delivers flowers to the Acropolis with her mother, and they swear to God that they witnessed a statue being taken off the Parthenon. I was really mad to hear that, and I told my parents. They in turn told the local Priest. We are powerless as it appears that the Ottomans are letting this happen."

"This is what I have feared." Alcibiades replied. "My cousin and I and some friends, we may have to go up there, beyond the guards to try to reason with them."

A worried teacher responded, "I heard that they are rough. My friend told me that a few Turks with access to the site who tried to intervene were either beaten up or bribed to stay quiet. I will come along with you. My Portuguese temper is no match for anyone." She winked.

"No, my dear, you live too close. You can be our 'spy' and keep me informed of anything you learn."

He took some tentative steps. He froze, yet the day was warm. Anamarci blushed.

"I, I…." He stammered, and quickly exited the studio.

Anamarci smiled and followed him with her eyes.

He returned. "Aren't you too young to be teaching?"

"Are you not too old to be hitting on a teacher?" she laughed, just a few days short of her 18th birthday and two years younger than the bearded Alcibiades, who had premature greys in the said beard. "My father owns the studio. I know ten languages and I enjoy teaching people. As long as we are in Athens, this relieves my boredom and helps me prolong meeting a proxenio, an arranged marriage!"

"I see."

"My mother is very traditional, but father wants me to follow my heart, always. This is like a compromise. Teach and contribute to society or meet the man of my mother's dreams." She smiled. Her eyes lit up further.

Alcibiades could not take it further, he ran from the studio, still trembling from his wordy encounter.

———◆———

The small group of Greeks, consisting of men and women, young and old, marched up to the Acropolis. The guards assigned to control the entry point were deep into tsai, cards, smoking and snoozing.

Some of the group surrounded the guards, while Alcibiades,

Eleftheria and a few others snuck their way in. In front of the Acropolis, they could see that Lusieri, and his men had erected scaffolding. A half-broken monument lay at the feet of the artist. He was startled to see them.

"I am sorry, but we do not allow visitors to the Acropolis." He yelled out in Italian.

"I am sorry, but we do not allow our Acropolis to be ransacked!" A forceful Eleftheria replied in the same language.

The artist walked to meet the group. He was no diplomat like the absent Earl who was back in Constantinople or the calm Reverend, who loitered in the background.

"Listen, take any more steps on this site and you too will become smashed like some of these ruins. Walk away now and I will pretend you were never here. Ignore me like a deaf person and I will have you banned from Athens, and not before you are whipped."

Eleftheria, Alcibiades, and friends were unmoved. Even when all the tradies, numbering 25 surrounded them.

"This is a final warning, Alcibiades and Eleftheria."

The two looked puzzled.

Lusieri quipped, "how do I know who you are? You take pathetic tours for foreigners. I know you have repeatedly asked the Turks to bring tours up here. It is I and the Earl who ensured your denial to enter the sacred site."

Alcibiades knew what was coming. It did not stop him from throwing the first and second punch and spitting on the fake artist. The pain to his fists was worth the effort. The bruises, well, not so much.

———◆———

Anamarci and her students did their best to patch up Alcibiades and some of his friends who were hurt in the ensuing scuffle by the scaffolding of the Acropolis. They were thrown out of the site, with the following words ringing in their ears, louder than tinnitus,

"The Ambassador will have you banned from not only Attika, but you will also be banned from mainland Greek speaking provinces, or you shall be killed."

Thanking Anamarci and her students, the cousins eventually made their way home. Two weeks later, Ottoman troops pulled up to their home with a letter for the two. They were now officially banned from Athens, ostracised, just as the con artist had predicted, in a 'Nostradamus' kind of way!

Alcibiades knew they would eventually end up in Constanta to study, one day. The ostracism meant that he would also look for other potential new homes where Greek was spoken and take the time to visit Calabria before arriving in Constanta.

On the day of departure, Alcibiades paid Anamarci one last visit.

"Please keep in touch. I, I…." He stammered.

She stopped him from completing his sentence. "I have some patriotic friends in Thessaloniki. When you finish your studies, I will connect you. Maybe you can all one-day help liberate our people."

He stepped forward; the classroom was empty. Finally, he acted on impulse and kissed the teacher. It had taken too long, and he knew it. The room suddenly felt like it was spinning as tongues twirled and hands moved across two bodies in one motion.

11

1803, AN ATHENIAN IN THE MEDITERRANEAN AND A SHIPWRECK OF TREASURE

AFTER ALMOST TWO YEARS AWAY going from city to city, town to town, the cousins finally made their way to Reggio in Calabria. "If only there was a 'frequent travel' points system, we would have free trips," they often mused as they fondly recalled their journey.

The pair had fled Athens with little money and made their way first to the Greek city of Ayvali, opposite Lesvos before slowly travelling down the Greek speaking coastline to catch a boat to Alexandria. Here their Greek and French language skills enabled them to work in hotels and hospitality. The large Greek community was vibrant and powerful, though a little unaccustomed to thinking of Athens as anything other than a backwater. Alexandria stood as one of the largest cities in the world, Athens was just a small city with significantly less Greek speakers than Alexandria.

The President of the Greek community had received a letter of explanation of events in Athens, from the family of Anamarci. She had hitherto expected their visit in Alexandria. She was the first ever female chosen to the position, a milestone in most countries. Yet in Egypt where the Greek Queen, Cleopatra, is fondly remembered, and where many a woman has ruled, this was barely mentioned as an issue by the cigar smoking men at the Greek Community Club.

———◆———

Early 1802, in Alexandria, word reached the President of the Greek Community that Lord Elgin would be sailing from Piraeus to take stolen treasures to Portsmouth, England.

The President had dealt in business with many a Greek merchant fleet and was told of this by the harbourmaster, Sappho as well as a businessman from Smyrna and his daughter. They had dispatched a message to Alexandria, explaining that the British apparently had permission from the Sultan.

"Permission, my Greek Egyptian butt….", her assistant said aloud as he smoked his cigar.

"Michalis, bring me the two young people who came from Athens."

———◆———

Sitting by the old harbour of Alexandria, the President welcomed the two fresh youngsters with a warm greeting, followed by an exchange of pleasantries.

"Look! Shortly, a ship containing 17 boxes of Greek treasures will depart Piraeus. I heard that you had some trouble at the Acropolis."

"Bad news travels fast."

"Thanks to the printing presses Napoleon left behind before he evacuated Egypt, we can print news quickly! However, I believe it was friends in Athens who told me about you two."

The cousins looked perplexed.

"Relax. You are amongst friends here. I need to stop that ship reaching Portsmouth. I am an old man, perhaps I will live another two or three years. If that is all that I have, I will devote it to stop such treachery from occurring."

"I see." Eleftheria approved.

"I need to stop that ship without anyone from Egypt being directly implicated. The French, the British are all over this place. The Mamluks and Ottomans are about to go to war over Egypt. It's best to avoid entangling any Greek Egyptians."

"How would two skinny young upstarts from Athens stop a ship, I hear you ask?"

It was a woman's voice.

Everyone turned from the view of the harbour as a woman in what appeared to be a hijab came into the light.

"I am Mona, and my great grandmother was Theodora, from the Cyrene. Some of my ancestors are from Apollonia. I can still speak some Greek words that I learnt from my giagia. I have a small boat and a small group. Thankfully, there is no shortcut around the Morea. The treasures must come via the Soranic Gulf, past Porto Heli and Spetses and to Kythera for supplies or at least to round the island of Aphrodite. Our job will get us close to the small ship and try to sabotage it."

"Won't it sink?"

"Of course. The treasures can lie at the bottom of the Aegean Sea. When Greece is free again, I am certain those treasures will be located. My small group has a diver originally from Kalymnos. They are the best at diving into the sea. As if they are fish or dolphins. The sea is her friend."

"What if anyone dies?" Alcibiades asked innocently.

"Then Hell will have some more souls to welcome!" The President retorted, continuing,

"Mona and her team are good friends of Egypt. We trade a lot, and we support each other in dealing with colonial oppressors. Importantly, they are designated protectors of the Greek ruins of the Cyrene. They are not hear for money, they are here for duty and honour. If this can happen at the Acropolis, it can happen elsewhere too."

The woman from Cyrene, Libya turned to the two. "We leave tonight, and we need you. In or out?

———◆———

The harbourmaster signalled for the 'Mentor' to leave Piraeus. Standing next to her was a teacher as well as her father.

"Anamarci, why on earth would some fool call a ship *Mentor*?" Numski asked.

"The mentality of it, is mentally insane," she explained. "Let us hope either Poseidon or the sabotage crew do their bit."

For days, the vessel struggled against the winds that the sea was conjuring up, while from Alexandria, Poseidon was assisting the small crew of a boat named, 'Rainbow Warrior' which was gliding fast, rounding Crete, and had seen a recent and ferocious uprising against the Ottomans. The crew was on track to arrive in Kythera before the Mentor would turn into the Ionian Sea and most properly be harder to locate again. Timing was everything for the mission.

On 16 September, after a number of days of struggling, the tired Mentor made it to the outskirts of Avlemonas. The depth of the sea was 20 metres. The time was 1.10 am. The crew of twelve was asleep, snoring loud enough to remind Poseidon of this group of barbarians. The First Mate was at the helm. A wee bit inexperienced, the vessel was drifting slowly as the sea was now calm and smooth. The First Mate was under instruction to pull into a port to obtain additional supplies. He kept searching the shoreline for signs of light.

—◆—

The Rainbow Warrior was as quiet as a mouse in a feta factory, pulling up close to the small ship in front of them.

The Kalymnian and the Athenian dived into the water with a bag of tools each. The Athenian had learned to swim and dive on the Attika coast. He dreamed of going to the ancient Games. He always hoped that modern Games could take place in Athens, where people from all over the Greek world could compete.

The divers made it to the side of the hull. The vessel was almost stationary. On the deck, the driver had eased up significantly to have a quiet drink and admire the calm of the sea. He always admired what the water could provide him. Unable to swim, he felt secure on board a ship, any ship and his only ambition in life was never to sink!

The water in this part of the Aegean was warm enough for the divers, who could dive in any type of waters. The crystal clear and clean water made it easy for the Kalymnian, who was just as adept in the water as out of it.

The divers made speedy progress, taking turns to support each other and smash pieces out of the wooden hull. The work was proving tiring when a dolphin made its way nearby, playfully watching and splashing water before continuing on its journey. The First Mate could see that a dolphin may have been causing the vessel to rock somewhat.

"Stupid fish," he yelled.

Meanwhile, the divers smiled and marvelled at the mammal.

"A good luck charm! He sounds like he is saying, 'Flipper.'"

As Flipper swam away, the duo completed their mission with several holes large enough to be breached, ensuring a slow enough sinking for human cargo get away safely. Soon the Aegean blue was penetrating the 'Mentor.'

The divers scrambled on their boat which almost immediately began to leave the vicinity. As the 'Mentor' began to capsize, the words 'mission accomplished' could be heard.

"Ok team set a course for Benghazi, our work is complete, for now." a woman's voice could be heard.

A job well done, may have also be due to the Elgin curse of ships sinking with important cargo.

———◆———

When a pig marries a rosy cheeked blonde woman of beauty and money, what becomes of such a union?

In the late 1700s, a broke man approaching the age of 30, in failing health would get you nowhere, save a potential ticket to the penal colonies…. However, if that broke man with poor health also had a strong education, a military rank of lieutenant-colonel thanks to his title, 'Earl,' as well as a stint as special envoy in Vienna and Brussels and another posting to the Court of Prussia; well, things would be different.

Gaining an Ambassador role to the Ottoman Empire would certainly make a wealthy upper-class woman, feel a certain heat in the wrong places. He courted Mary Nesbitt, a courtship that her family approved of, and which her status demanded.

She was also swayed by his benign project to mould and sketch monuments, artefacts, and buildings. Greece, no, not the poor folk who inhabited Greek lands, ancient Greece was a worthy place to be in. The art, Byzantine churches, sunny weather, and ruins were enough to tempt anyone from Scotland.

Mary naively believed that the benign work of her husband would prove to be an inspiration for all artists back home. She was also hooked on the story told by her husband and his home estate architect, Thomas Harrison.

They were building Broomhall House and wanted to adorn the large estate with copies of art from the Greeks as well as any real pieces. The House itself was taking on elements of Greek style architecture to complement British designing.

It did not take long for the adventure to the Ottoman Empire to recede in enthusiasm. By her second year in Constantinople, she longed for the long winter days, the mono dimension of people in her circles, the English language, and the weeks of no bathing for the commoners.

Over the three years in Constantinople, Mary gave birth to three of their children. Despite the demands of being a mother and a wife to an absent Ambassador who would spend chunks of time on business chasing his pet project, she still managed to help arrange shipments of his stolen treasure. This would, perhaps, make her aiding and abetting, a thief, for it was her fortune that was paying for his passion project.

In 1803, they started their return to Britain, with the children sent via the Mediterranean and the couple making their way through the continent. She was 12 years his junior, some would call that a 'cradle snatcher.' A nice title to compliment his stealing habits.

———◆———

12

1803, REGGIO

FINALLY, THE COUSINS TRAVELLED ALONG the African coastline, stopping for several months near the ancient and Byzantine Greek Cyrene. The pair integrated themselves with the small, remaining Greek speaking population of nearby Benghazi, another city once founded by Hellenes. Cyrene was the birthplace of Eratosthenes, the mathematician who calculated the circumference of earth and invented the Leap Day, while a number of philosophers lived there including Socrates' pupil Aristippus who founded the School of Cyrene. Saint Mark the Evangelist was also born there, as was the Bishop Zopyros who attended the famous Christian Council of Nicaea in 325 AD.

This stop gave the cousins added nostalgia. A fear that what had happened in Athens, with the brutal removal of artefacts, as well as the overlordship by Ottomans, must end. To preserve their culture, they needed a free Greece.

———◆———

As the ship sailed through the Messina Straits, Eleftheria shed a tear. She was back home, her original home. For Alcibiades, it was a bittersweet feeling. Longing to be home in Athens, this was his paternal grandfather's town for a few years in the early 1700s. His pappou had found his way here after stabbing a number of Ottoman soldiers one night in a fit of rage. He had to flee.

His pappou once told him, "the Greeks of the area once dominated the economy and social life through their overwhelming
numbers, commercial dominance and achievements in mathe-
matics, science and philosophy. It was the Greek heartland. Now
Rome treats us as foreigners in our land."

In many ways, Calabria was also like this for Alcibiades.

As they travelled in by horses from Reggion, they passed signs
that proclaimed, "Roghudi this way," "Pendedaktilo" this way, "Vua
this way" and the key sign they had come to find, "Galliciano."
Until recently, Calabria was a Greko speaking heartland. The heart
is perhaps reduced in size now, but the history and Greek soul have
had a significant ripple effect across southern Italy, a region known
as Magna Graecia, 'Greater Greece.' This was arguably the first use
of the term 'Greece' anywhere in the world, taken from an Epiros
tribe that had once migrated to Italy.

This would be their home for the next year until they could
move to Constanta for further studies. And to ascertain what help
may be forthcoming from Greeks in that part of the world.

———◆———

Travelling around Calabria and not knowing Italian would be a
problem for anyone. For Alcibiades, it was a breeze. For not only
were the Calabrians expressive in their body language, especially if
you piss them off, most could speak Greko or understand the dialect. He in turn could speak to them in Greek.

It also helped that he received two letters from Anamarci, including one explaining that she would be travelling to the Griko
speaking areas of Apulia. Her father was tasked with the duty
of investigating feasibility of setting up trade opportunities by
Athenians.

"Greece will be free. One day. It also means we need to be ready
to trade with our cousins in Italy." She wrote.

Alcibiades did not need to be invited to Apulia, he interpreted what he wanted to interpret. The letter was 'all Greek to him anyway!'

As the year suddenly became 1805, Alcibiades found his way to Apulia.

13

1805, APULIA

ALSO KNOWN AS PUGLIA, IS the home of dozens of Griko towns and Griko speakers. Their dialect was the lingua franca of the region until recent centuries, not too dissimilar from Calabria.

It soon became obvious to Alcibiades that he would need to go by stealth to every town, drink in every drinking establishment until someone confessed to seeing an Athenian Goddess.

He was more enthusiastic about the towns than his mission to study in Constanta this coming year and soon became friends with most of the friendly Griko speakers he encountered.

One day, sitting in a square listening to Griko and having a coffee was a treat. The shop displayed a poignant sign: 'Ettosu milume o Griko,' the language which likely went back to the ancient Hellenes who dominated the region.

Apulia had Alcibiades' heart racing. The mainly flat landscape is covered with olive groves, ensuring an easy path for traversing. He truly felt at home. He felt as though he were in Attika thanks to the olive groves. The proximity to the Ionian Islands and the Morea helped keep a steady trade between Hellenes. The Ionian was the one place in the Greek world that had finally regained a semblance of independence thanks to Russian intervention, becoming self-governing under a joint Russian-Ottoman 'protection.'

"How long would that last? Until of course other European

powers make an attempt on the Ionian prizes." Alcibiades opined to himself.

One elderly Griko woman in Calimera told him more about the history as he visited a church. She had understood by his dialect that he was not from Apulia.

"….Our region remained under Constantinople until 1071, temporarily again 1155 – 1158. With the fall of Constantinople, Trebizond and then Morea by the 1460, many Greek speakers came here and to Venice, ensuring the Greek presence remained prominent. It was not until the Vatican, disappointingly, forced a change of Greek churches and monasteries two or three centuries ago to Catholicism, which precipitated a decline of the Griko language."

Alcibiades admired the monuments and a Greek museum in Calimera, together with Griko murals and poetry on the walls when he toured the town.

As he travelled across Salentina, he marvelled at how the Griko towns have a medieval feel meets sandstone. Some of the towns he rode through on his donkey included Martano, Castrignano dei Greci, Soleto, Sternatia, Martignano, Castragano and Zollino where he was welcomed as a 'local.'

At the latter destination, the Athenian stopped at an orange sweet shop for fresh bread. After a long day of travelling around, this was a nice experience. The owner may have struggled with Alcibiades' Greek as he peppered him with questions, before finally understanding.

"Bellissima gineka/woman." He smiled and pointed behind the Athenian, who turned his head.

"Why is your jaw on the ground young man? Please pick it up." The shop owner laughed.

Anamarci, true to form was not flustered.

"I had a feeling you would pop up. Come, I have two more days before Papai, and I are to leave from Brindisi. By the way, is there a problem with your jaw."

The two embraced as the sun set.

———◆———

The next day, Anamarci provided Alcibiades a letter.

"I want you to learn as much as you can in Constanta. I promised to connect you to some friends, and I imagine that you will be much sought after by exotic women! And by men who seek the liberty of Hellas. That must be your mission, your goal. Who knows, maybe one day I will find you, instead of you searching for me. We can write our own chapters in a book of love!"

Alcibiades remained silent, knowing that it would be the final night he would see his Goddess. He knew what was to be expected of him. His name implied adventure and destiny, just like the Athenian General he was named after; the General who jumped ship before the Sicilian Expedition had landed in Syracuse, 2000 years earlier.

A tear was shed.

A bottle of wine from Lesvos was opened.

Candles were lit and sins created as the full moon left a glow across their entwining bodies, as two bodies found a common purpose.

———◆———

14

A NOT VERY GAI PARIS BACK IN 1803 AND BEYOND

As THEIR HORSE AND CARRIAGE bumped up and down on a cobble stone street, the smell of perfume permeated the air, alongside baguettes and African cigarettes.

"This is wonderful, my Earl. You really are a pearl. It's such a pleasant country. Yes, no one can speak English, yet the way they dress and smell and express themselves. I wish I could live here."

The chubby man nodded in agreement to his wife. He was content that he was not only robbing from the Greeks, but he also cradle snatched this beauty and had made his way to the cultured France where Napoleon was at peace with Britain after his butt had been kicked in Egypt.

As they stopped in front of the hotel, there was a commotion. A poor person handed him a newspaper. He shuddered at the thought that he could have been a poor person had it not been for Mary, his wife. He wanted to cleanse his hands.

He looked at the paper. Dated, 18th day of May 1803.

"Guerre declaree."

He muttered, "that Napoleon, who is he stirring up trouble with this time?

"I can answer that sir." A stranger called out.

"That would be delightful," replied the Earl.

"Napoleon is going to war with the English."

"Again?"

"Oui, oui!"

"Drats."

"Indeed, this is bad for you, sir. You will need to follow me. I am Chief Inspector Clauseau. We have some questions for you at the station." A tall, skinny man with a moustache, glasses and a cape flashed his badge.

"I am not your enemy." The chubby Ambassador yelled.

The Chief Inspector offered sympathetically, "I know. You are an Ambassador. You must be one very dumb British person to want to travel to France at this moment, sir!"

"We were at peace just this morning." Bruce mansplained.

"Every morning turns to night. I am afraid, an Ambassador is the highest possible person we can capture, I mean question...."

The Ambassador looked defeated and reluctantly obliged, trudging off slowly with the Chief Inspector. The sweaty little monster would get his wish to spend time in Paris, albeit not the way he intended. He walked slowly, a wee hobble from the weeks of travelling and sitting on his large behind.

For the next two years, Lourdes became his new home. Snails and wagon wheels were a staple of his diet. His pregnant wife remained in Paris to work for his release. She stayed with the chubby one's close friend, Robert Ferguson of Raith. A dashing man with longish hair, red cheeks who served some time in parliament and also the military.

A pregnant married woman, who was married to his dear friend. Nothing untoward could possibly occur, or could it?

———◆———

1806, Somewhere in Paris

Thunder and rain bore down on the home shared by the bachelor Robert; he chose to avoid the temptation of French brothels, lest he bring home a disease, for he was a careful man and as a careful man he cared about his health and wellbeing. The lonely mother again, felt cold and afraid one night as the thunder crashed. The lights of the candles dimmed. They gave each other comfort, until that comfort was no more. It was a night of passion instead. Which soon turned into another, then another and another. Passion from two desperate people in a foreign city hostile to Britain.

The child she bore in Paris had an untimely death a few months later. Pregnant again, magically by the Earl, she departed France.

By 1806, Napoleon finally allowed the former Ambassador to leave for England. The following year, the married couple got a divorce. To make up for not gaining anything from the divorce, save for the custody of the children, the little monster sued his one-time friend for the affair he had with his wife. Making a cool 10,000 pounds. Not a bad little earner, a timely earner, for the now bankrupt chubby man, this would surely help him out from his current predicament.

Goddess Athena had a nice little laugh from the top of Mount Athos, Makedonia. Some would say karma. But what type of karma? For despite the fact the Earl had suffered, more of the antiquities had made their way to England, only to be trapped inside crates that were gathering dust. The dust starting to dull the delicate shine of the priceless antiquities. The Earl and Mary had paid for rescue divers to salvage what they could from the Mentor sinking off Kythera before the Greeks could.

———◆———

Rewind 1803-06

As Bruce rotted in a French prison far from trendy le Gai Paris, the gnawing feeling that his wife was having an affair, the shipwreck, and now dealing with gastro, the little monster felt cursed. He absolutely hated the snails and frogs being offered as food!

Fortune did smile on him somewhat. Stolen fortune to be exact, as 44 crates had arrived in 1803 via a ship from Kythera courtesy of the salvage operation. Upon hearing of the delayed news, his mood took a slight upward curve and his gastro seemingly corrected somewhat by 1804.

15

1808, CONSTANTA, IS THERE A DOCTOR IN THE HOUSE?

ALCIBIADES AND HIS COUSIN HAD long since left their rebellious and adventurous ways behind them. Alcibiades had two more years remaining to become a doctor. His cousin was denied the privilege. Her gender was the drawback. Disappointed, she studied for and became a nurse, working across the Black Sea. She had returned to Constanta to announce she would be joining the medics in the Tsar's military.

"Why cousin, why?"

"When I was in Marioupolis, I was impressed at how the Russians admire Greeks. The city was founded under Catherine the Great, no relation to Alexander, in 1776 for Greeks and by Greeks."

"Ok, now I am biting."

"They have this potent drink that people drink, as if it is tea. Vodka.! Then they say,

Ola kala, kai panta kala (always good, forever good). With the clink of my glass on my first day there and the downing of another vodka drink, I started to feel very much at home in Ukraine. On a bright Sunday afternoon, I had found myself in a small town, Sartana, just outside the city. By chance I could hear music in a building. I poked my head inside through the door/window to listen to the music being played. I found myself at a local Greek wedding. This was the second day of the wedding, the feast day. True to the nature of Greeks and their generous hospitality, I was immediately invited in to sit at the main table to enjoy as much local cuisine and vodka as I could possibly consume. The only problem being that most of the people at the wedding made it their mission to have a drink with me. One cannot be rude and refuse a drink in Ukraine!"

"Haha, please tell me you did not fall over Elcftheria." He laughed.

Chuckling, she shrugged her shoulders. "This was a taste of Greek life in Ukraine. A wedding where most of the guests were Greek descendants — many still speaking the old dialect, I almost felt like I was back in Athens. At the end of my afternoon, with a tummy full and thirst quenched, I ended up at the home of a lovely couple. Of course, the hospitality started all over again. Oh, and through the couple I met a bachelor friend. We are now engaged! Our plan is to marry within two years and eventually settle back in Galliciano as goat and natural produce farmers."

The cousins embraced, happily. Joyously. Alcibiades thanked God for such wonderful news. He was happy to hear the news and opened a bottle of wine that he had been saving from Serbia.

"We intend to marry when we are ready. He is a sailor in the navy, having spent time in the Mediterranean, which he enjoys! He will return home in 1810, and I will be waiting for him. Until then, I will work here as a nurse then return to lead my life and raise a family.

1812, Constanta on the Black Sea and a Rendezvous

As the birds circled and chirped at the dock of the Black Sea, on the growing city of Constanta, a smartly dressed Alcibiades hurried to the church hall. It had been four years since he had been to this church hall, which also served as a profitable tavern to keep the congregation and friends/parea happy between prayer. Even now, he barely made it to church, let alone the tavern. Preferring to focus on his role as doctor and having spent two years in the Russian military. He occasionally received a letter from his Goddess in Athens. He never opened them. This time he did. It was the vodka, the vodka pushing him closer and closer to open the letter staring at him with the faint scent of Milano perfume. A perfume that was popular in Athens amongst single women. He could not resist the temptation.

"Dear Mr. Handsome....." and the letter went on until it came to the concluding paragraphs.

"Please make the time to listen to the man who wrote about his travels in his 1811 book. He is presenting in Constanta and my two friends Melina and Solon will be there. They spent time in Athens a few years ago. Remember, I wrote to you about them."

Alcibiades was intrigued, though he deliberately had not read many of her letters lately due to a heavy heart being far away from where it should have been, the final paragraph fortuitously stood out.

Now he was moving swiftly, opening the door, late as always.

Mr Edward Daniel Clarke was presenting 'Travel to European Countries.' Half of the audience looked Greek. In the back row, a couple sat, transfixed on the door. They had been waiting for a doctor as Clarke was lecturing,

"I witnessed a grown man, a Turkish officer who broke down crying. He could not believe that the British were destroying a monument that was of historical value to the whole world. Sculptures were stripped from the Parthenon. I watched in horror as the South Metopes was ransacked. Large blocks were cut into smaller ones. I feel ashamed to be a man, to be British. I wanted to complain." He explained.

"Of course sir, just write to the Ambassador who is looting in other parts of Greece." He continued.

A question from Melina, "Mr Clarke, why would they chop up something that is that precious?"

"As it is cheaper to store and transport. You see, he was a frugal man, using his wife's money as he had none of his own. He did this not just in Athens, also many other sites of Greece too," he replied.

"Mr Clarke, what else did he 'borrow' that you are aware of?"

It was Alcibiades standing by the door, as a hundred curious eyes turned to meet his saddened eyes.

"At least one Doric column stolen, along with a large number of figures from the pediments, fifteen metopes from the rear of the temple 56 blocks of Panathenaic frieze, statues also from the Propylaia, the Nike Temple and Erechtheion; add in dozens of inscriptions, statues, artefacts, broken marble and more. There is likely more! Remember, he has other artefacts from Greece too. He is no art lover; he is a monster."

Many in the audience were openly weeping. The Priest was consoling some of the elderly.

"That is not the biggest tragedy."

People gasped. *What could be worse?*

"He has an estimated 80 crates of stolen items, all sitting at his home. Last year he unsuccessfully tried to sell them to Westminster. Ironically, I heard that Napoleon is planning to make a bid in the next year or two. His sponsor into the French military was a high-ranking Greek French officer and he himself has family from the Greek part of Corsica, people who originally came from Mani. It is said he may gift it back to the Greek people."

The crowd roared in approval. Cheering the name of Napoleon.

The speaker provided more anecdotes about his travels and then closed the session with his visit to Beirut where he again met many Greeks. He was given a standing ovation.

Alcibiades and the couple from Constantinople lingered.

"We need to talk." Solon explained to the doctor, who nodded.

Sitting by a tavern looking out to the Black Sea, which remained dark no matter what time of the year it was.

Alcibiades started first,

"Constantin Ypsilanti was a regular here when he was in Constanta. He ruled (a Greek P on behalf of the Sultan. Greek people, mostly Phanariotes from Constantinople rule Wallachia and Moldavia, Romania."

"How is this Alcibiades?"

"Under the Ottomans, there were areas of that empire that were either self-governed or controlled outright by Greeks. In fact, the early Ottomans are more benign than many have given them credit for. Greeks prospered as they generally had a good handle on commerce and merchant trading. In Constantinople, Greeks continued the level of schooling and education that was the standard practice during the Byzantine epoch. In an area of the great city called Phanor, you could find thousands of Greeks. A class of bureaucrats emerged. They became known as the Phanariotes. Wallachia and Moldavia have been the host to a number of noble families. One of these was the Constantinople nobility of the Cantacuzino in the 1500s."

He took a deep breath

"Nicholas Mavrocordatos was the first Phanariot to rule and proved to be loyal. Nicholas ruled until 1730 and his son took his place until 1769. The key elements of rule by Mavrocordatos were the promotion of Greek culture; This included Greek fashion, increased promotion of the language, costumes, and Hellenic manners, whilst building a number of Greek Orthodox churches. Nicholas wrote a Greek novel, *the Leisures of Philotheos.* Importantly, he abolished serfdom and sought to have his people educated. It should be noted that the Greek culture was already noticeable prior to the Phanariot era, now it was elevated it to a level that was below local culture. By the late 1700s, Russia had gained a presence in these lands due to their temporary occupation. This helped the Phanariotes further; soon they were starting to support the emergence of a Greek secret revolutionary society that was being whispered about. Ypsilanti ruled until 1805 and the Russians have been here ever since, gaining sections of the Danube and also Moldavia between the two rivers Pruth and Dniester. The Tsar will bring his troops home soon, meaning a Greek will again rule as he has to be a man that the Tsar will agree upon. Ypsilanti, God bless his soul, also has sons and they are involved with Russia." Alcibiades concluded his 'lecture.'

"I will never again go to university when I have you Alcibiades." Melina laughed, and she was joined by others listening.

"My point is this feels like Greek land. I won't lie to you; it is possible that Greek freedom may start here." Alcibiades added to his verbal essay. "Something that interests you."

"How do you know we are interested in Greek freedom?" Melina asked.

"The letter. It was Anamarci who has also previously introduced me to contacts with the Russian military. That is how I took on a junior officer role, and I met people who will be leaders in an uprising. Change is coming. Ypsilanti tried a few years ago. The Cretans have tried many times. It's been attempted in the Morea. Her father is a well-connected businessman. They know people everywhere."

"Look Alcibiades, we empathise, and I think we will get there. However, there is a more pressing, urgent matter than liberation of humans!" Solon pitched.

Alcibiades looked on, trying to supress a frown at them.

"We want to liberate the marbles. The stolen treasure that a monster has taken. We know you tried, twice….." Melina was hastily interrupted.

"I don't know what you are talking about." He looked around, out of habit.

"Alcibiades, when we arrived in Athens, we met your friend. She took me on a tour you had laid out for people in the past…."

"She owes me commission," he laughed.

"I was devasted by what I saw at the Acropolis when we bribed the guards to let us visit the site. She explained to us what had occurred. I could not sleep and eat. She described who was behind it. Then it dawned upon us, we met the pathetic excuse for a criminal in Constantinople." Melina explained.

Solon interjecting, "he was very likely obtaining a cheap firman, a fake, most likely misspelt and with typos. We could never forget this man. He looked disturbed and he was in the building where my uncle has his fabric shop. The man he was dealing with is known for forgeries. Forgeries!"

"We cannot let this man hold our prized, sacred possessions. We have spent the last two years in Thessaloniki scheming of ways to seek retribution, when Anamarci mentioned we should travel here. She also knows Mr Clarke."

"I, I…." taking a deep breath. I am sorry, but the adventurer, the man you think I am, was, HE IS NO MORE!!!!!! Please, look elsewhere for support."

The immediate silence, even a nomisma coin being dropped on the other side of the room could be heard.

The couple looked at each other, painfully. Sadly.

"Look, stay. They make wonderful sarmale cabbage rolls and jumari. I have a tab. Enjoy, drink up and be happy." Alcibiades stood up and made for the door.

Melina too stood up, and in the tradition of party goers on Delos in ancient times, she jumped on the table. Only it was not to move her hips. She commenced reciting a poem, *Freedom.*

Our land
Our freedom
Oh take me to the seed of redemption
Oh treat me to a revolution.

Our journey
Our ways

Oh come now time,
Oh come to our aid.

Our fertile
Our earth
Oh why shall it hurt,
Oh how can it end?

Our people
Our liberty
Oh what a pity,
Oh it came for too soon.

A couple of tears were shed by her beautiful words. Melina was hoping that freedom would come to all whom she touched. The owner of the establishment however, kindly asked her to come down from the table. She may have been petite and light, but he valued his tables and their 'freedom.'

———◆———

Alcibiades had stayed, facing the door with his head bowed. His black hat was trying not to fall off, just like the pieces on the Parthenon. He caught the hat and placed it on his dark, scruffy hair.

"The winds of Poseidon are changing dear doctor." It was Solon, "we will visit here again on this date in one Gregorian calendar year from now, same time. Please don't keep us waiting on your Greek time."

Alcibiades, with his purple umbrella, exited through the door as a loud clasp of thunder was heard, lighting up the Black Sea. A strong gust of wind and rain followed.

———◆———

Melina and Solon spent their year based out of Pella, on the Thermaic Gulf, near Thessaloniki. This was the birthplace of Philippos II and his son Alexandros. The Star of Vergina had its home here and the ancient Hellenic Kingdom of Makedon was anchored in this small, yet historic town. The city founded by King Amyntas, had most of its artefacts taken by Romans when the Makedon empire ended in 146 BC. It was rumoured when a certain Scotsman had nibbled on a few items here, he was eventually chased away by goat herders and Arvanites. The couple were determined to avoid the fate of Pella, and to protect Athens and her treasurers at all costs.

Two weeks before their rendezvous with a reluctant Alcibiades, they rode out on two beautiful horses. They galloped at full flight, as it was forbidden to ride horses if you were Christian. Melina had carefully packed their supplies, which included a letter from Anamarci in Athens, with the instruction, "open in Constanta only."

1813, A rendezvous in Constanta

Alcibiades had never again given further thought to the two eccentrics, those annoying two strangers. His life continued as a respected doctor by day. During the evening he enjoyed the company of males, going to the gymnasium and boxing wherever and whenever he could. He liked to tell people it was to relieve the dullness of sitting in his office six days a week and then sitting in church every Sunday. His one moment of pure pleasure was the stop off at his favourite tavern by the Black Sea. Without fail, he was there for a very long lunch and a drink every Wednesday. He returned to work inebriated, though he never took patients in the afternoon of a Wednesday.

It helped that his tab was a trade-off for providing free medical services for the owners and workers. The Greek owners felt compelled to look after their employees, who consisted of men and women from the Balkans. They had garnered a reputation as an employer of choice with extra money earned by working on a weekend.

Alcibiades sat in his corner, toasting to himself for being "voted the best doctor in Constanta." A poll that only he and his imagination regularly partook in. Finishing his meal, Alcibiades made his way to the bathroom. A small shack in a far end room that was cleaned daily for the convenience of patrons.

Melina and Solon walked in. They looked at the pocket watch that Solon carried around. Looking deflated.

"I knew he wouldn't be here."

"Melina, my love, he is a hard-working doctor, he is probably at his surgery. Why not return this evening and wait for him? Perhaps we can go for a walk along the harbour to catch our breath."

The couple walked out the door, heading for the harbour in front of them to take a stroll.

Alcibiades took his time. He did not like the smell of a public toilet area and he had drunk a lot. His urine was as long as the Danube. He shook it off and washed his hands, something not too common for the common people. He strolled to the door and thanked the owners with a smile and a nod.

Then bam!!!!

He fell to the ground. His new red suit from a Persian tailor roughed up and dirty, before he even had a chance to wear it for long. A hand reached out to him.

"Sorry about that, I entered too quickly."

"It's fine, I know a good doctor," he chuckled.

"As do we, Alcibiades!"

The doctor peered closer at the thin man. "How do you know my name?"

"It is Solon and Melina. We thought you would not show. I dropped my pocket watch, I was here a few minutes ago…. And we raced back to collect it as it is from Thebes. A priceless item from an aunty."

"And you know my name because….?"

"We met you here a year ago, remember? Mr Clarke, the stolen marbles!" It was Melina's turn to reason with him. Alcibiades rubbed his well-groomed head, trying to shake off the stupor.

"Oh dear, what are you doing here again? I can have you banned."

"Come now good doctor, you mean you didn't intend to meet us here?"

"NOOOOOOOOOOOOO. Oxi vre!"

He began to reach for the door. He needed a holiday. Life was monotonous in Constanta. Turning,

"It is a busy time for me. I will shut down in December for a few weeks. We can take an adventure then if I feel up to it."

"That is far too long…."

"My terms or none! You may stay with me in that period, just do some chores and keep noise to a minimum. No sex on my couch."

The couple couldn't argue with that and decided on the spot to take up the unexpected offer to see the year out.

<hr>

When December came around, Melina called the two men to the table. She had a letter that needed opening.

"Gentlemen, this is from Athens, and it is time to read what has been written."

Slowly opening the letter, she poured over the contents of the letter and skipped the non-essential points before settling on the following.

"When you meet again with my Alcibiades, know that he is a compulsive trainer, a good soldier, intelligent, a doctor, if in need, and a damn good kisser, which hopefully no one else ever needs! I have an important person you must meet in Venice. He is well connected and condemns the looting of the Acropolis. What is more, I have made arrangements through my father's business contacts for his assistant to meet you there in January. We have provided supplies and money for the trip you said you would take. My suggestion is that you wait until Italy to explain the plan. Please keep in mind, despite the cool appearance of Alcibiades, my father tells me that he quickly gained fame with the Russians for his brutal abilities in any conflict or situation. There is a growing movement in Europe that will lead to Odessa soon. Alcibiades will be a man who is sought after. Make sure he returns from your adventure and goes straight to Odessa. If I remain unwed, I will meet him there. That part is a surprise."

Melina shook her head and smiled for revealing that part of the secret. Alcibiades suddenly seemed incentivised.

16

1815, BELGRADE

IT HAD BEEN A HARD slog trudging to Belgrade with snow and minor frost bite setting in. Alcibiades and his companions had taken a slow travel journey though the Balkans. The heavy winter and his desire to take a holiday after nonstop continuous working meant, by the time they arrived in Belgrade, the colder months had given way to a warm summer.

Melina had communicated to Athens that their journey was going even slower than a tortoise in a race against the hare. On the day of departure to Venice, Melina fell ill. The Athenian doctor examined her, determining pneumonia and respiratory illness would keep her bed ridden for weeks. The weeks turned to months, by which time the reborn revolutionary spirit of Alcibiades had been extinguished as he opened a practice with Solon as his assistant.

Once again Alcibiades felt comfortable and in workaholic mode, in a city that was welcoming and delightful. Once again, he welcomed a new year, 1815, with Solon and Melina when he received a letter from Athens.

The next day he dashed. Telling his companions, he would return in a month.

True to his word, Alcibiades returned, smiling, tanned and upbeat. He explained that he was in Corfu, though his words were in short supply and few more details would be enticed from him. His main coat smelled of Milano perfume which seemed to linger. He also had one look, a happy look.

Once again, Melina fell ill, and the intended departure was delayed again by months until she was strong enough to travel. She would also need to convince a settled-in Alcibiades to abandon his practice again to head for Vienna to meet the mysterious 'assistant' that Anamarci had alluded to in her latest letter.

——◆——

With summer having drawn to a close, 1815 was a time of mistakes for the French under Napoleon, the companions packed their scant belongings for Venice.

At a tavern in the heart of Belgrade, amongst the bathhouses and bazars, rum was consumed, and toasts made. As the night drew on, Alcibiades' boasts of more freedom for occupied peoples were not received well by a table of Ottoman soldiers.

"Sir, maybe it is time for you to go," the friendly Serbian barmaid suggested.

"Yes loudmouth, time to go home." It was one of the soldiers, almost daring Alcibiades. The soldiers were in no mood to play nice, having just lost a large number of troops in the Second Serbian Uprising. Milos Obrenovic and Marashli Ali Pasha were now negotiating the future of Serbia which had the local Ottoman troops on an edge.

Alcibiades and Solon had treated many Serbian injured fighters, in the short uprising and had no love for the local occupiers. The doctor was goading the soldiers, teasing them for being unable to defeat 'goat herders.'

The entire table had had enough and without warning jumped on the doctor and began attacking him.

"Is that all you got," laughing, Alcibiades used his superior Russian military training to block, kick, punch, block. A form of fighting that the Russian military had brought back from their

Asian provinces. Solon and Melina too tried to join in on the circus, however, the doctor had taken care of himself.

He took a small wad of cash from one of the bloodied men and gave it to the barmaid.

"This is for their tab." He wiped away blood and walked out the door with Melina and Solon in tow.

"Hey, what is your group called? Do you have a name or title?" She tried in vain to learn who the group was.

The group hurriedly jumped on their horses and rode toward the city exits. Perhaps it was confidence or the alcohol, perhaps it was karma. As they inadvertently rode in the direction of the Ottoman barracks, a company rode out to meet them. Not for a friendly visit.

"Melina, Solon, you both turn back and make your way to the Greek Archbishop. If anything happens, I am sure they can help. No matter what happens, you must ride to them now. Go."

The duo, reluctantly, galloped away.

Alcibiades jumped off his horse, ready to meet his fate.

———◆———

Days later, Alcibiades woke. He was in a bed in a mosque. The striking artistic features and Arabic writing on the lower ground was in stark contrast to the tavern he last remembered being at.

"Kalimera." An elderly man offered, a doctor.

"You have been in a coma for a short period. The Imam has a good relationship with the Christian equivalent, and I have been allowed to care for you until you are well. A few more days and you will be as good as new. You sustained some head injuries and broken ribs and a broken hand. Being in a coma, you have healed well thus far from the broken bones part."

"Thank you, doctor."

"You are welcome doctor! Listen, the soldiers are here outside guarding. I can buy you a week of recovery here. As a fellow doctor and the good relationship, we have with your church, we will find a way to get you out of here. We are tired of the uprisings and deaths. The church has sent for an important Phanariot. He will either get you out of here diplomatically or by force. Understood?"

"Thank you, I will never forget."

———◆———

As the week rolled on under the kind-hearted nature of the old man, the soldiers kept a watchful supervision. The old man had once lived in Constantinople, and he learned the art of medicine from Greek medics who never once treated him poorly despite their differences of religion and culture. They were colleagues and medics; all owed their allegiance to Hippocrates.

During the First Serbian Uprising, the Christian church and mosque stepped in to help civilians caught up in the fighting, helping people irrespective of faith and affiliation. Not everyone approved of the support and kindness, to a doctor, his only thoughts were helping people.

An SOS had been made to the church from the mosque to help rescue Alcibiades. The SOS had found a receiver in Michael Soutzos, who arrived on the penultimate day before the handover of the patient to the soldiers.

As a well-known interpreter for the Ottomans, Michael arrived with a small posse of non-Serbian soldiers to demonstrate neutrality.

Michael, dressed in a long flowing silk dress with a regal robe and a long bushy black beard, dismounted from his horse, having ridden almost without break. He and his men had come immediately from Wallachia. The men were part of John Caragea's personal attachment, the Prince of Wallachia, allowing them to ride horses wherever they wished in Ottoman occupied lands.

"Men, I am here to take possession of the Greek doctor."

Laughter. "You may take his body when we finish with him. He is to be sent to our barracks, for 'special duties.' Maybe come back next month.

In one quick movement, the soldier boldly proclaiming what the special duties might look like, suddenly had a huge hand wrapped around his throat and a sword in the other ready to strike.

"It's been a long ride. I am not asking, I am telling. My authority exceeds yours. Do not test me, do not try to talk me down. Your men behind me with swords drawn, my advice to you is to lower them. My men will cut you to pieces. You can't even beat Serbian farmers. Last chance."

Slowly, the men lowered their weapons. The soldier who had now turned blue due to the said big hand was coughing and spluttering. The Turkish doctor rushed to his aid with his kit bag. As did Alcibiades, a call of duty.

The soldier was rolling on the ground.

"It's ok, we will help you," the elderly doctor explained calmly as he turned to take some water from his bag.

The elderly man suddenly dropped to his knees as if he had been the one who nearly choked to death. A khanjar dagger had penetrated his chest. Alcibiades screamed at the soldier and caught the elderly man who was now coughing and spluttering blood. Soutzos threw Alcibiades a small blade, in an instant he stabbed the soldier over and over again, until Soutzos pulled him away.

Alcibiades looked at both men. What should have been his death, was now the death of two others. The soldiers turned and moved out slowly, disgusted by the action of one of their own for killing a defenceless old doctor.

Alcibiades carried the old man back to the mosque, where he was met by volunteers who had witnessed the exchange. Tears flowed.

17

1815, WALLACHIA AND A GREEK PRINCE

JOHN CARAGEA HAD RULED WALLACHIA since 1812, as a Prince or Hospodar appointed by the Sultan. A large bribe did not hinder his cause. His work in creating effective measures to address the bubonic plague outbreak was hailed, limiting the deaths to 70,000.

His men, a mixture of Greek and Albanian, were only too happy to take in the escapees and bring them to his country residence.

Entering a quaint humble, well defended estate, they were struck by the greenery, livestock, and the mountain in the background.

Melina and Solon had been picked up at the Danube and joined the riders for their next 100 miles into the territory of Wallachia.

The trio stared at the mountain as the sun had set; taken aback by its sheer rugged beauty and what appeared to be a moving shadow in the distance.

"If you are searching for a mythical being, you won't find him there." A large man dressed like a Sultan rather than a Greek prince interrupted their thoughts.

A hesitant smile from the group. "Come my children, you are amongst friends here. Time to end your journey with a feast."

The group, devoid of high sustenance and meat, devoured every bit of pork, beef goulash and vegetables brought to them.

"My friends, I received a letter from Athens. Alcibiades, I know about you."

"I'm flattered, uh, er…." He stumbled.

"I intend to live my life out in a free Athens. I am a Hellene at the end of the day, despite ruling in Wallachia. The Sultan can still take back the provinces here at any time." The Prince explained, before continuing.

"Recently I raised taxes. Most of this revenue will end up with men who will do the right thing for liberty. As we speak, there is a small organising federation of intellectuals, military men, diplomats, businessmen who are growing in strength in Odessa. Alcibiades, when you finish on your current adventure, they will need you. All of you have a role to play. Until then, I am most intrigued by what you intend to do with the marbles. If you bring them safely home to Athens, I will provide you with monetary resources to keep them safe and secure and to return as many to the Acropolis as possible."

The trio looked at each other.

"For now, considering you took out a soldier, the Sultan will send men all over the Balkans looking for you. However, Michael will put in a good word and in a few months, you will be forgotten. Until then, you will eat, study, train here. Doctor, we will send you locals who need medical attention from time to time. When it is safe again, we will escort you to Venice and you will have as many supplies as you need."

Melina looked at the host. "Are you really helping us? You are too generous. Why?"

"Liberty. Here I am, wealthy materialistically, I am educated as I am a Phanariot from Constantinople. I love and enjoy Wallachia. The Sultan does not make life too difficult for me. Yet, no man can truly ever be happy without liberty for himself, his family, his people, his patrida. Athens and Constantinople must be the home of free Hellenes. I do not think we can reverse 1453. However, I do think we can renew the light of Athens."

Solon interjected, "first we have a task to fulfill, the stolen marbles."

"Let's all drink to that, giamas!" It was the Prince, smiling. "Say, you should use this time to think about a name for your group. Are you a mob, resistance, entertainers, lovers? It is always good to have a moniker, especially if you become known to history some day!"

Melina shrugged. "Maybe the Fabulous Three or Four? Who knows, I am sure we will eventually settle on a group name."

More drinks flowed and stories were exchanged as the hours progressed until the sun was peeking through the mountains before any of the weary eyes shut. Our weak travellers fell into a slumber.

———◆———

As the new year melted in with the snow, the trio bade the Prince farewell, who ensured they were well stocked up on local wine. They rode out in small convoy, their travelling companions for the next month with Venice as their destination.

At the head of the small contingent sat the chirpy, chubby giant, Michael Soutzos. His grandfather had been Prince of Wallachia until 1802 and he was now one of the most senior interpreters and diplomats for the Ottomans. A Phanariot with revolution in his heart.

Melina asked him what Venice was like, "was it a little Hellas on water."

"Why does everything have to be Greek!" Solon chided.

The Phanariot chuckled, "in a way, as it has been influenced greatly by Greek speakers."

"How is that?" she asked.

"Oh no, he is going to make a short story long," Solon groaned with a twinkle in his eye.

"I remember sitting in St Mark's Square, admiring what was in front of me. Such a romantic city. There was a gala, lots of colour, people enjoying themselves and the horses. The famous horses of St Mark's Square, which symbolise triumph, were in fact stolen from Constantinople around 1205 by the Venetian military who had been on their way to a Crusade. Instead of pursuing the Crusade, they used their 'stopover' to loot this great city. Venice was the pre-eminent maritime power." Soutzos explained, then continuing for the group,

"The four bronze horses are said to have been the work of a Fourth Century Greek sculptor and had adorned the Hippodrome of Constantinople. The Venetians and Latins found themselves in control of the capital for over 50 years until retaken by Greek forces. This act of treachery and the coinciding loss of the horses began our long road to ruin, which eventually ended with defeat to the Ottomans in 1453. The holder of these magnificent statues represented world influence. Napoleon took them in 1797 when he defeated Venice. The statues were returned to Venice when Napoleon was defeated last year." Soutzos sighed.

Solon offered, "is there a pattern that when these horses are taken away, the power who loses the horses is the one that has been defeated?"

"Maybe! Anyway, we all know the Venetian Empire controlled many Greek cities and islands, often joining forces with the local Greek population to take on the Ottomans. A famous example is the 24 years the Cretans and Venetians held out the Turkish forces until 1669. This was an incredible fight of bravery; neither side was willing to surrender. Crete is an example of the influence of Venice in Greece. The Venetians built higher buildings, small or no balconies and the streets were paved with arches. Fortresses can be found across Crete. They also introduced different colour schemes to a home setting. Across many Greek lands you will come across some Venetian architectural influence." Soutzos concluded.

"What about in Venice?" Melina asked.

"You can feel the history and the splendour of Venice, however, if you blinked you would miss the Greek connection. I was there on diplomatic business, and it was by chance that I stumbled upon a Greek church. I remember how excited an Italian woman became when I explained I could speak Greek. I think she was trying to tell me she was of Greek origin when the smell of latte and gelato took me away to another piazza," he joked.

Continuing, "Venice was either founded in 421 AD as tradition tells us or in the 600s, when the small communes banded together as one community under a leader called the Doge. Most of the Italian peninsular during the 500s – 600s was under the control of Constantinople. An early and important Doge was Orso Ipato, a Greek who was born in Heraclea, Calabria. The Doge reported to our Emperor, however, Venice was in essence an independent state whose foreign relations and some taxes were controlled by Constantinople, though our influence receded several centuries later. When Constantinople was defeated in 1453, and in the lead up to that disastrous event, many Greeks migrated to Italy including Venice for protection against the Ottomans, becoming a key ingredient to what became known as the Renaissance. Many writers brought their own work as well as the classics to usher in the Renaissance. Soon, there was a Greek library; the first printshop in the world, was created to reproduce Greek texts and the teaching of the Greek language. Cardinal Bessarion, a Greek Catholic born in Trebizond, donated his entire collection of Greek manuscripts to Venice. This resulted in one of the largest Greek libraries in the world."

By now the entire posse was listening intently before Alcibiades chimed in. "The man who invented the modern printshop in Venice, Aldus Manutius, was deeply immersed in Greek culture, created the Neo Academia focussing on the classics."

"Correct," the Phanariot continued. "By 1580, there were over 15,000 Greek people in Venice out of a population of 110,000. In 1539 an official Greek church was built and whilst I am not entirely sure, this is probably the Church I had stumbled upon in Venice in the Castello area. They always say about Greek and Italian relations,

una fatsa, una ratsa, which means one face, one race. This has tra-
ditionally referred to the Greek people in Calabria, Apulia, Sicilia,
and Basilicata, not Venice. However, one has to spend some time in
Venice and various parts of Greece to understand we have a similar
historia. An influence that goes both ways. I'm glad that such a historical city as Venice has a Greek connection…. Now if they could
just return those horses, per favore!"

Everyone laughed, to the point that one of his men fell out of
his saddle. Alcibiades tended to his gashes and soon enough, the
group was on its way, keeping to a small river on a low-lying mountain. There was nothing but sunshine, slightly melting snow caps
and the occasional wild animal roaming freely. The type of freedom that the Greeks yearned for.

18

1816, ENCOUNTERS FROM VENICE TO SWITZERLAND

WITH THE ODOUR OF THE canals of Venice in the air, the escorting companions called a halt. The leader placed his hands on the shoulders of Alcibiades.

"You may not know it yet; I will see you again in Odessa and eventually in a free Athens."

The doctor chose not to respond, yet he understood the meaning as he turned to face the warrior. He nodded.

"I heard that Lord Byron is drawn to Venice for its Greek and Armenian connection. I think you have chosen well," Soutzos smiled in a Nostradamus type of way, as if he knew the future, or the present.

A number of white birds flew above, settling on a tree nearby.

Once goodbyes had been exchanged, the trio rode on to the odour of the canals.

———◆———

As the group took a gondola to search for a room for board, Melina reached into her carry bag for a Milano perfume-scented letter. In Wallachia, another Milano perfume-scented letter had made its way to the trio from Athens. The instruction was the same as a previous letter. *To be opened in Venice.*

The letter contained a few pleasantries directed mainly to Alcibiades. She smiled and was about to pass on the letter to the doctor when she stopped on a paragraph that needed to be read, aloud.

"Palazzo Mocenigo, will be your place of residence whilst in Venice. There are two people waiting for you. One is Eleftheria and the other may be a renown poet."

"Palazzoooo Mocenigooooo, si si, Bellissima, fantastico." The excited gondolier began to sing as they passed the Ponte di Rialto (Rialto Bridge). *"I am a sixth-generation gondolier, and I will never shed a tear.... Without a chandelier, you will have no fear."*

Alcibiades now clutched the letter and smiled as he drowned out the singing of the Venetian. The Milano perfume scent now permeated his nostrils.

———◆———

Somehow, Alcibiades had an inclination this day would come. Sitting by the Grand Canal near St Mark's Square and the four stolen horses, the Palazzo had been home to seven Doge's of Venice. Now it was hosting a 'special guest' from England and another from the other side of Italy.

Eleftheria had been waiting. She flung her arms around her cousin and then introduced herself to Melina and Solon.

"I trust that your journey here has been pleasant. All of our family was worried about Belgrade; now I am relieved to see you in front of me again. Our good Lord has blessed you."

She touched the cross adorning her neck on a silver necklace, before adding,

"Come now o' weary travellers. There are rooms for all of us. They have already been paid for, as well as any expenses you incur. In exactly one hour, we are to dine with our sponsor!"

The group was intrigued. Alcibiades did his best to extricate the information from his cousin, to no avail. She did explain that the man lived with his two mastiffs, 14 servants and had started a writing project called, *Don Juan*. "You will eventually meet him. Eventually."

The only real information he could obtain from Eleftheria was that her Greek-Ukrainian husband was staying behind to look after the farm. Only one of them could make the journey, though he did escort her as far as Ravenna, one time stronghold for Byzantine Greeks.

An hour later, the group reconvened in a dining room. Dozens of candles lit the room, a room decorated with all the splendour and lavishness expected of a Venetian palace.

There was one chair that was empty.

Alcibiades made some funny remarks at the empty chair. Clearly not believing that anyone will turn up.

Then, an angelic sound floated into the air. Someone was reciting poetry of the highest order. Not since Odysseus had to be tied to his ship, has anyone heard such beautiful words.

A man with piercing blue eyes, and wavy red hair, strolled into the room.

The hair on the back of Solon and Alcibiades' neck stood up. Soon everyone had stood up.

The man smiled and motioned them to sit. He went to each person and gave them a hug.

"B,B,B,B…." Alcibiades stammered.

"What's a matter, donkey got your tongue, o Greek doctor?"

"BYRON!"

"Well, if you all gonna sit there shaking in front of a harmless English man, I dare say what you will do when you reach Paris!"

"Paris?"

"Yes, and the real Byron will ride out with you. We have a small window of time and a short time frame." The Englishman manages a broad smile.

"You mean, wait, you aren't the great Byron? Alcibiades seemed rather disappointed.

"I am his assistant; I am blessed to look a wee bit like the lad, and I have a good enough voice to recite his poetry. I am here months in advance to prepare for George to visit."

"George?"

The man could not suppress a laugh. "Yes, few on the continent know his real name, George Gordon Byron, Sixth Baron Byron."

"And this Lord George, he will actually physically help us?" Alcibiades asked.

The Englishman looked deep into the concerned eyes of Alcibiades before answering.

"He has spent a good deal of time castigating your intended target in British media, across the high society and in prose. The pillaging of monuments is not why we tread on this precious earth. Therefore, he will come with you, perform the deed, and get himself here to Venice when the task is completed. He must, as he has to work on an Armenian dictionary and of course, he will be writing plenty of poetry. He fully intends to be in Greece in the next few years, Missolonghi, I believe. Freedom is near for the Hellenes. And hopefully for the marbles too."

The group finally settled their nerves over wine imported from France, part of the collection that Napoleon owned, which Byron had procured. The man explained that his defeat last year had probably set most of the European entities back a generation, with the loss of men and resources. One thing for sure, Napoleon offered to buy the stolen artefacts, he explained.

"Imagine if Napoleon had succeeded. The artefacts would be in the Louvre now and we could try reasoning with them. It is possible enough pressure would have seen them returned to Athens. Sadly, the British Museum is set to control them now unless you reach them. The fight is just beginning. Once you have a full list of what has been stolen from the Earl, and a copy of the fake firman, we should be able to 'negotiate' or otherwise."

Byron's double continued as he gazed at the quizzical look upon the faces of the group. "One other thing, we have hired a man who helps in sticky situations. He is from Marseilles, though his father is Cypriot. He converses in French and Greek, and unlike me, has lived in Paris. He will meet you in Versailles. After a brief stop in Geneva."

The group drank, sang out of tune, and enjoyed the night, which soon became morning.

"By the way, you people should consider a name for yourselves, a moniker," Byron's assistant suggested.

"Not only are you a good companion and assistant, but you are also a wise fella. Something to think about over more wine! As for a name, yours is?" The assistant nodded at Alcibiades, then continued singing, before adding, "Rooney."

———————◆———————

The small posse had long since left the comforts of Venice. Winter is not always the best time to be riding through Europe with the occasional frozen road, snowflakes, and rain. After weeks of almost non-stop riding, they had made it to neutral Switzerland. The reason for the neutral stop was apparent by the HUGE smile upon the faces of the entire group. Not necessarily, the picturesque Lake Geneva surrounded by mountains, greenery, and an abundance of hiking trails.

More because of a certain Byron; and then of course Mary Shelley and Percy Bysshe Shelley. The two were in their honeymoon period.

There is no better way to describe what it means to meet the most famous, charismatic, and charming poets; with a social conscious added in.

The one night that the group spent there, is a night that will never be forgotten. A slightly inebriated yet witty and intelligent Byron waited for them as they entered a large home, the Villa Diodati at Lake Geneva. A younger image, and a more handsome image, of the man they had met in Venice.

Before pleasantries had been exchanged and weary bags unpacked, wine was passed around and poetry recited. Alcibiades also contributed with his own brand of poetry to engage with the mood. Something taught to him by a man he met in Athens, a painter from Lesvos, Theophilos Hatzimihail. The man explained he intended to teach his children and their children, especially if any carry his full name, the art of Greek folk painting. He wanted to learn more about Athens but yearned for his beautiful homeland during the visit.

Alcibiades stood up, hoping to impress the poets and all sundry who were gathered around.

Home
I know a place that is paradise.
A home to be precise.
A paradise that is home, a welcoming home.
My home, irrespective of where I may roam.
My island.
From the sunrise to the highland.
My homeland.
A homeland scattered amongst the sand.
From the mountain to the sea.
My island can let you be.
It will keep you guessing.
A blessing.
For my home will always welcome.
No matter whence I have come.
My heart is there, a true forever.
Lesvos, if only I could, whenever.

Everyone clapped at this audacious bid to recite the poem from Mytilinis Smyrna, a poet from Lesvos. Alcibiades beamed, as wine continued to flow. He wanted to leave his mark amongst some of the biggest names in Europe before the inevitable return to their journey the next afternoon, after siesta of course.

19

PARIS AND THAT REPROBATE BRUCE; AND PIERRE, A PIERRE A FRIENDLIER FRENCHMAN

FRANCE HAD EXPERIENCED THE FRENCH Revolution, the takeover by Napoleon and six wars with Europe. The final war, the One Hundred Days War, resulted in the end of his reign as a combined force of a million Europeans came out against 200,000 French. The city had kept its charm, with a feeling that, one day, Versailles would be known the world over. Until then, it remained in touching distance of the Capital and another stop for the group.

Checking into a non-descript hotel, the crew had just one task at Versailles; meet Pierre Leventis who had ridden up from Marseilles. Byron decided to recount at the communal dinner, his version of Greek presence in that part of the Mediterranean. When Byron spoke, everyone listened, it was like experiencing a night at the Epidavros.

"One of the first Greeks to make it to the edge of the Mediterranean was a powerful and heroic man, and I'm not talking about me here," he offered, "rather, the great Hercules. This powerful giant built the *Pillars of Hercules* on either side of the Gibraltar Straits to signify the supposed geographical limit of the known world. Herodotus tells us that another Greek, Captain Kolaios of Samos, and his crew mistakenly sailed past the Pillars of Hercules and landed in the region of Tartessos in Spain in the Seventh Century BC. The Greeks exchanged goods whilst working on their tans. Kolaios and his crew returned to Samos with Iberian silver, minerals, and stories of potential new trading lands. A number of trading settlements were created. Then during the Greek colonial epoch, the Phocaeans established the colonies of Emporion and Rhode in Spain, then…." He was cut off by a new voice to the conversation. Heads turned.

"The Phocaeans established Massalia about 600BC. A local story tells us that Protis from Phocaea was invited to a "coming out" event by a local King for his daughter. Protis was your typical Adonis or Hercules looking Greek; the girl fell in love with Protis, and they were given as dowry the land in what would become Massalia." It was Pierre, a French-Greek man from Marseilles, explaining what he knew.

The stranger continued, as Byron slowly rose to place a hand on the man's shoulders. "Massalia developed as a leading city and was the first Greek colony in the region to reach a population of over 1000. When Belisarios and Constantinople conquered, it helped us retain the Greek language longer. Massalia also established colonies such as Olbia where I was born, Antipolis, Monoikos and Nicaea. The growth of Greek merchant trade in the Ottomans era enabled the remaining light of Hellenism to grow again as Greek ships moved to our ports. France owes the Hellenes for introducing olives and wine to France. Anyway, Byron and I talk too much history. I am Pierre, and I am a Frenchman and a Hellene, here to help you all."

The group was glad to welcome Pierre to dinner. A man who knew what the Hellenes were owed for their contribution to the history of the continent.

"May I ask, do we have a name or something stylish to refer to ourselves?" Pierre asked of the group.

Melina shook her head, and the group paid no further adherence to the question.

———◆———

Early next morning, as birds chirped, wearing thick woollen coats and sipping tea to warm up, Pierre laid out the plan.

"In Spain, your Earl would be called *El Stupido*. Where, on this earth, he would return to a nation where he was imprisoned and his ex-wife was shagging his best friend, not to mention the death of his baby. El Stupido does not seem to have the best of luck, and I learned that the British accused him of stealing from a dead man, a Phil Hellene, and a classical scholar, Mr John Tweddell."

Angrily, Alcibiades crushed the spoon in his hand. His muscles had never receded from his training days.

"That dog. Mr Tweddell was a lawyer from England with a genuine love for Greece in his heart. I met him before his death in Athens in 1799. He had a French artist always with him as he travelled Greece making impressions of the landscape and in particular Mount Athos. What would the pig want from such a good man?" Pierre asked.

Pierre continued as everyone listened intently to the scruffy voice. "Turns out our 'hero' pig heard about the drawings, all of which were in significant detail and artistry and worth a few pounds. His French artist also took detailed sketches of ancient sites. The little pig, as Ambassador issued an order for the drawings to be sent to him. These drawings had been held in trust by Prokopios Makris on behalf of the Levant Company. Our hero Ambassador sent those home to Scotland for his own use. Most of this came to light since last year. Robert Tweddell, the deceased's brother sued for their return and has written a book about the situation. Edward Daniel Clarke, whom you met in Constanta I believe and a range of English editors and the Earl's Ambassadorial predecessor, have called for their return."

Alcibiades, eyes wide and ready to explode. "Let me guess, he is saying he removed them to protect them from barbarians!"

"Turns out some have been lost, mostly to water logging or a ship that went down at sea. Unsure." Pierre replied.

"See, further indisputable proof that he is a THIEF. T H I E F. We can teach him a lesson he will never forget." Melina, smiled. I know just what we need to do.

The conversation paused, just enough for the angelic voice of Byron to recite. It was another recital pertaining to the theft of property to lands beyond the continent. There was not a dry eye in the room, except for the battle-hardened Pierre.

———◆———

The road to Paris was easy. The group galloped passed the Palace of Versailles and took the one road that said, "Paris and that reprobate Bruce." Or at least that is how Melina read the sign in French to the others.

On the outskirts of Paris, ten miles away, the little monster was now settled with his second wife. His small estate paid for from the proceeds of crime, the crime of the century. A century which was only 16 years old.

It was a sunny day in April, hovering at 20 degrees. A heatwave by the standards of Scotland! The sudden burst of good weather had drained the sweaty man by the early evening. Kissing his wife goodnight, grateful that this one was not cheating on him like his first wife. He turned down the lamps. He noticed one of them did not have enough oil at its base.

"Must punish the servants for this tardy indiscretion," the monster thought to himself, shaking his head in dissatisfaction.

On the perimeter of his estate, the group had arrived and fanned out. The signal would be 60 minutes after the last light was flickering no more. That way, the couple would be drowsy, and their natural defences would be low.

As the time marched on slowly, some of the group realised that their hearts were racing. Byron was reciting poetry in his mind and Solon was starting to have second thoughts. "Is this the right thing to do," he wondered, as the group was set to break into a dwelling by force.

With no further time to ponder. Pierre rose. He moved like stealth in the shadows. The pitiful servants quarter outside, passed the outhouse, small and decrepit, was full of snoring. Pierre felt for the class of people who remained in servitude all over Europe, and for slaves around the world. He saw enough of it on the ships that came through Marseilles. His father had been part of a small fleet equipped by an American to help intercept slave boats. One small fleet was not enough to redress the imbalances in the world. It did, however, equip Pierre with the skills he needed to undertake such enterprises.

Eleftheria and Solon entered the property, their role was to cover the main entrance should anyone hear commotion and try to enter.

Alcibiades and Pierre picked the lock using a Russian tool and were soon joined by Byron and Melina to make their way up the staircase.

They stepped lightly for fear of causing a commotion that would wake the servants in the sardine can which was called the 'servants quarter.' Each step on the velvet carpet made the heartbeats of the Greeks grow louder. For Pierre and Byron, despite their big hearts, they were cautious, focussed, and sure of their task.

According to the information that the Frenchman had obtained from a source in the local Planning Commission, the master bed-room would be just over the staircase. They had counted 10 steps. Alcibiades, full of adrenalin and unable to contain himself, burst into the room. Seeing a bed linen of gold, he threw a small dagger at the top of the bed.

Melina screamed.

Byron grabbed her and placed a soft, well-tended hand over her mouth. "Save that for Solon."

"Quick Byron, it's the next room." Pierre whispered and tried to quietly open the adjacent door. It was locked, and two weary heads were asking themselves behind the safety of the door what the devil was going on.

Not being in a mood to negotiate, filled with rage and hate, Alcibiades did what the Russians had shown him. Run at the door with your shoulder.

Bam! He bounced back and tumbled, comically, eliciting nervous laughter from the contingent.

The quick-thinking Pierre picked the lock and stormed. He was followed by the group.

The very *brave* little monster pushed his wife in front of him as Alcibiades barged passed the hapless woman. Alcibiades was the only one who chose not to wear a face covering, reasoning that he had nothing to hide, it was the thief who should hide. He grabbed the man who was now sweating profusely.

"Do not be a crazy Cretan, which I know you are not." It was Byron in a slightly altered voice. He stepped forward and threw a hood over the captive. Melina did the same with the woman, reassuring her that no harm would come to her as she sobbed. Melina put an arm around her and whispered that everything would be ok, for her.

Pierre ran down the stairs to see if the others had noticed any movements from the servants quarter. Nobody stirred. And why would they? Over worked and underpaid for ungrate*fool* masters.

Alcibiades now slapped his prisoner around. One punch, "this is for Athena." Next punch, "this is for Saint Philothei, she is a Patron Saint of my city. By stealing you also insult a just Saint."

Byron had to restrain him. "Easy lad. You need to calm down. Let the emotion flow later."

Alcibiades ignored him and pulled out his knife again.

"Mr Thief, on behalf of all the marbles you have stolen, I will now take a marble from you. Fair is fair, please spread your legs for me, come now, spread…."

Pierre had trouble hiding a laugh and suppressed it with a plague style cough.

Alcibiades was like a man on a ledge now. He was going against the simple plan, tie them up, find out where the marbles are, get the firman and leave. No violence. Byron had mistakenly believed that some of those pieces would be in Paris, hence letting Alcibiades take his party trick a bit too far.

The knife was now inside the night garments of the sweaty man. Alcibiades said what they were all thinking, "Mrs Earl of Elgin, you probably do not need a beach when you have this wet whale to play with."

The group laughed as Alcibiades composed himself, controlling his emotions now. Though he had made a small cut at one of the private marbles on exhibition to the houseguests.

Melina chimed in, "I still think we should take one of his marbles and only return it if he fesses up to what he kidnapped or marble-napped!"

"I did not steal anything…." he snapped.

"Alcibiades, every time he lies, cut part of his marbles please….." Melina was forceful this time.

Alcibiades smiled and made a movement with his knife. The man with the potentially soon to be missing marble sensed the threat.

"I see what you want. You think I stole the marbles from the Parthenon. You know who I am. I am respected, educated and known all over Europe. You will struggle to attain what you want. Besides, I sold it to the British Museum…."

Alcibiades sent the pointy end of the knife back to where it was most comfortable and moist.

He shrugged. "If I did not take them, the Turks would have."

Byron interjected. "Such a liar sir. The Turks generally leave the sites and churches alone, save to convert a few to mosques. They much prefer to take boys for the janissaries. They occupy Greek speaking lands. You sir were a guest who raped and pillaged their connection to their ancient, learned, and sacred past. You are nothing more than a barbarian."

"I had permission from the Sultan," came a now trembling reply.

"You had permission from a forger. Nothing more. Two of our people caught you in Constantinople in 1801, you were too cheap to 'purchase' a fake 'firman' in either Greek or Arabic/Turkish." Byron addressed the facts to the sweaty Earl.

"I love the classics…."

"You love yourself only," Byron reminded him.

"I want to protect the Greeks, not harm them." He retorted.

"See these people here, they are Greek." Byron pointed.

"Um, he can't see with the black hat on his head." Melina interrupted.

"Good point my friend." Byron smirked. "Listen, these Greeks disagree with you."

"We certainly disagree, you bastard!" came a few replies.

"I feel sorry for the bastard." Melina added.

"Eh? No way do not fall for the sweat and lies. This is the same chap who bought his way to the rank of Captain in the military, same chap who used his first wife's money to take, take, take, and take again from Greece. Then this little monster tried to sell what he stole in 1806 to the British Museum; he could not get a buyer. Decided to divorce his wife and sue her lover to make a bit of cash. He also humiliated her by divorcing her in England and Scotland and the unheard-of tactic of divorcing in parliament. Parliament should be for national business. He should know that, for he has been a member, technically since 1790!" Byron explained.

"Ok, ok, a moment of weakness afforded by my upbringing in church in Thessaloniki." Melina replied.

"He does not know the meaning of forgiveness and redemption; he is owed none. Not from us, nor his maker. He is an embarrassment to Scotland." Alcibiades scorned, still holding his knife.

The little monster was moist around his groin area. His satin garments were leaking.

Alcibiades placed a hand on the man's throat. "For God's sake man, tell us what we need to know."

Shaking. "In the study next door, you will find a yellow envelope. It contains a firman."

Melina hurried off to the room next door with a lantern.

In a frail voice from the sweaty one, "you are too late, Byron. Parliamentary Committee has made a decision. I was represented by my dear Reverend, Philip Hunt. They know I took the marbles legally. The marbles have been signed to them tentatively, and I have already been paid! Admittedly, half of what I paid for originally. That is the true crime."

Angrily, Alcibiades yelled without a thought of who would hear, replied, "the true crime is, you kept these treasures in FUCKING crates. And your Priest lied to the Committee. The same man who stole minor artefacts himself from a dig at the Acropolis and elsewhere in Greece. He is a thief like you."

The sweaty one had the gumption to deny it. "All of the crates are either at my estate at Broomhall House or at the British Museum by now, ready for official sign off by the parliament.

Byron turned to the group.

"We have the 'firman' and I think I know where the marbles are."

Melina, felt in her heart and spirit that they were in London, and whispered that to a concurring Byron before he returned his attention to the sweat machine sitting in front of him.

"Thomas, you have a choice, I can leave Alcibiades here to finish you off like one of those poor statues you desecrated. Or you can keep your bloody mouth shut about this little visit. The man who will slap you in the face in a moment is based here in France. Should you even attempt to tell anyone what has happened, who we are and what we intend to do, he will find you."

Alcibiades moved the knife back into place between his private parts. "I really think we should take one of his personal marbles and only return it when we have recovered the stolen artefacts."

Pierre, "I think we should head on out; we have a long ride ahead to the Channel. I think he is telling the truth and if not, his personal marbles, small as they are, will end up sitting atop of Big Ben!"

One by one the group filed out, though not before Pierre broke his nose to provide the Earl a new look, that of an ancient Greek or Roman statue with a chiselled off nose.

As Pierre did his deed, Byron whispered at the bloodied head, "you worked out who I am. If it had been my choice, I would have let them do as they pleased. The Greeks will be free soon you miserable fool. You have caused pain and suffering to these people on the eve of their freedom."

"The Greeks, they are not even descendent of the ancients. They are too stupid to beat the Turk. The Sultan still controls a large empire," the bloodied fool spat.

Byron replied loudly, "the Sultan is the sick man of Europe. Just like you, except you are not only sick, but you are also a filthy man. Unworthy."

Byron spat at the man and walked out. "You sully the great deeds that Grant the Scot did in the dying days of Constantinople. Now, as rebirth approaches for the Greeks, you should have used your influence to help. You would have been remembered fondly. You were a little monster in childhood, now you are just a monster."

———◆———

Somewhere in Odessa, a group of men had their ears burning.

Sitting around a table in a small home on a main street, the group of men were writing and planning in the newly acquired head-quarters for the Φιλική Εταιρεία, Friendly Society (Filiki Eteria). The name in English becoming a misnomer for there was no friendly sign on the front door to give away the secret revolutionary society. They had no intention of being friendly to the Ottomans, they just wanted a free Greece.

A number of Founding Fathers and leadership gathered around the table, included Nikolaos Skoufas from Arta province, Emmanuil Xanthos of Patmos and Athanasios Tsakalov hailing from Ioannina. Joined at the table as they wrote out their commands was the reliable, Panagiotis Anagnostopoulos, born in Andritsaina. They were reading correspondence from Michael Soutzos and Alexander Ypsilantis, both well-known across Europe.

The Society was growing with names being tapped across the Balkans and Russia. The fearsome Theodoros Kolokotronis, Odysseas Androutsos, Dimitris Plapoutas, Laskarina Bouboulina, the angry Priest Papaflessas, the bishop Germanos in Patra and Byron were names being discussed today. Soon priests would be called upon to administer oaths to would-be revolutionaries.

Behind the men, one word was written on the maroon wall, *Patrida. Homeland.* Another wall to the side offered the following word, *Eleftheria. Freedom.* Similarly, to the stolen marbles, the Greeks also needed a homeland and liberty of their own.

———◆———

The race to thwart the sale and official exchange was on. The group made it to Calais after a week of riding. No boats were due to go out for another week.

"It is probably wise we rest and recover a wee bit. We need to properly plan out the next phase. We won't be attacking a pathetic thief this time." Pierre reasoned with the group, who all needed a breather. If we are caught, we may well be sent to Melbourne or worse.

Pierre then set off on a journey through the neighbouring province to find an old friend who served with him in the time of the French Revolution. The friend had been a visitor to Westminster, and always talked about the Thames and how beautiful it was to sail down the old markets and the medieval pubs. He would recall the poor treatment of lower classes who would be brutally shipped off to penal colonies on the other side of the world. Irish political prisoners being forced to join low level criminals in a dangerous journey to Botany Bay, a place where they had dispossessed harmless Indigenous peoples who had never seen these white ghosts before. His friend was fascinated by the British and at the same time looked down upon some of their practises.

"Anyone who would trade wine and snail for a cold, cold beer on a rainy day has rocks in their head! And it rains there all the time. It's why they have no need to bath, they can just stand outside for that." The friend would often muse.

Pierre found the friend in Ablainzevelle and hurriedly asked for an audience.

"For a bottle of wine and the answer to my question."

"Go for it Joan." Pierre smiled.

"Which village held out the Romans the longest?"

"I think our old Training Sergeant gave us that one, it is of course, the indomitable town of Alesia.

"Now Pierre, what do I owe this honour?" Wine hit the table and people talked and sang by a crowded bar.

———◆———

Pierre rode back to the group after two days. Aside from bringing back some wine and potentially syphilis from another stop, he had some answers. His friend had spent time at the British Museum and Westminster and drew up some detailed outlines and provided guestimates of guards, measurements, and anything else he could think of.

The group went over the plans again and again. They would have one shot, one quick window of opportunity if they arrived at dawn. They would have to return to a getaway vessel; and they would need to make a decision. The museum or the Parliament? Which of these held the precious items?

———•———

The destination was London. A city that had become fashionable, wealthy though with a huge class of poor, illiterate and 'undesirables.' Despite their loss in the American Revolution, British stocks were high, and the navy was now the biggest in the world. Another reason why speed was of the essence.

They say Paris is the *City of Dreams.* It is likely London is the theatre where it all happens. With almost 2000 years of history, London is a city where more nationalities under the sun are represented than anywhere else save for Constantinople, Alexandria, and Rome. It is where you can be and achieve whatever you want. London had a history of welcoming Greeks. From the Roman times to medieval times, Greeks occasionally ventured to the city on the Thames. One of the most prominent Greeks to have visited was Emperor Manuel Palaiologos in 1400 when he was trying to rally support for his battles against the Ottoman Empire. During his visit it is probable that he would have heard only the sounds of old English, in a city that has an array of greenery and architectural feats from the Victorian and Edwardian era.

As May approached, a rumour had reached Joan that the parliament was several weeks away from officially ratifying the purchase of the marbles. It was important that their venture from Calais commence without delay.

———•———

Just like a boxer or a Graeco-Roman wrestler in the last round, it had come down to this. For Alcibiades, the theft burnt deep inside of him. The memory of a precious Acropolis being vandalised by an apparent upper-class thief of an apparent country of culture.

For Byron, he had become synonymous with tearing the reputation of Bruce to shreds. He may not have been born in the Greek speaking lands, yet if you poked his veins, you would find Hellenic blue blood.

Pierre negotiated for an appropriately sized vessel that was fast and adept at cruising shallow water such as the Thames.

Each person aboard had a motivation for being there. The Captain was Irish, who was mystified by the Acts of Union of Great Britain and Ireland which came into effect in 1801, often complaining bitterly about the English. His small crew was a rag tag group of men from France, Ireland, and America. There was no love for the British. Added to the mix were men who had escaped from the Ionian Islands in the previous year after being held as political prisoners. Jack and Jimmy, two men who objected to the takeover of the islands by the British in the previous year, were captured after they raided a British military command post. The British accused them of repeating these 'offences' across the Ionian Islands and in the Mediterranean when under the employ of Napoleon.

Pierre had explained that Byron would personally compensate each man for his involvement. On the surface, the motivation did not appear to be money.

The Captain was thankful for all contributions and had just one question. "Does your group have a name?"

"Name?" Alcibiades shrugged.

"Yeah, you know like a Magnificent Seven or Dangerous Hellenes?"

"Not yet Captain, but I am sure it will eventually arrive in our thoughts when we least expect it, or over some wine!" It was Solon with a smile.

20

WELCOME TO LONDON,
HAVE A NICE DAY

THE BOAT, WITH THE RIVER Thames on either side, made its way unmolested, passing the entry point to the relatively new Port of Tilbury. A group of men, dressed in what could only be described as rags, were excitedly kicking something along the shoreline.

"Is that a severed head they are kicking?" Alcibiades joked.

"Appears as though it is some type of circle. These workers are from the docks nearby. Must be a way to release steam. They work far too many hours for low pay. Not much in terms of benefits." Byron sighed.

"Whatever they are playing, it seems enjoyable. Maybe England has a new sport? I do hope their work stresses are eased. In Constanta, my fellow medics and I formed an informal association, a united bunch to discuss issues in our profession." Alcibiades explained to Byron.

"I see. The hard-working industrial lads in Manchester, a United Manchester, have created what is called a 'trades union,' and what some of us call a philanthropic society. These men need that, otherwise my 'class' of aristocrats will continue to work these people to the bone. It has caused a stir as frightened aristocrats and printers do not understand why it is useful to help workers, not work them to death. I fancy this apparent union is months away from being formalised and ready to stand up for low paid workers." Byron offered his insight to the Athenian, who absorbed the information into his thoughts.

The vessel continued into the small port, where they moored on a chilly day. There they paid their duties to the Port Commissioner who inspected the boat.

Byron dressed up as a first mate and did most of the talking, explaining that the crew was in training and learning how to sail across the Channel and the British Isles with a view to running commercial operations in a few months.

"Well then, best of luck to ya lads. I think these cigars and bourbon from Napoleon will do me nicely for the day." The Commissioner, with a pipe in his mouth was simultaneously frothing and spying the women onboard.

"What about them? Is there a price?"

"Not for today Commissioner, they belong to our master who lives nearby I'm afraid."

He was about to open his crooked mouth, when Byron offered another bottle of bourbon and a copy of a book. "I came across this interesting read. Do you read much?"

"I was the first in my family to finish school, I can read!" he snapped.

"The ladies love it; it is poetry by a man named Byron."

"Fancy stuff. I have a lady friend whom I will visit this afternoon, she will enjoy it. She can read too."

Byron handed over a copy. "The poet has also signed it from what I can gather. I think your friend shall enjoy it immensely."

"She better…."

"She will, trust me." He smiled.

And with that, the Port Commissioner was on his way, taking his foul-smelling breath with him.

———•———

Pierre huddled with his key conspirators. "Let us keep a watch on his office, when he is gone, we slip out and head to the Rainham Marshes. Very few people are aware of this location, thanks to George, we know that there is a concealed series of narrow, stable passages that will take horse drawn carts. There are several that will be waiting for us. Thankfully, it has been dark and foggy. It will help give us the cover we need to remain undetected there and back."

It was Byron's turn, "I have a special treat for us when we reach the marshes. Just stay mellow until then everyone."

The two men from the Ionian Islands were asked by the Captain what was the point of difference of the islands to other Greek lands.

Jack leaned in, cleared his throat after a swig of whiskey. "It was a poignant Venetian stronghold for about five centuries, though few Venetians moved there from Italy. Napoleon brought the Venetian Empire to an abrupt end almost two decades ago; their impressive maritime territory eroded first by the Ottomans and then Napoleon. For the Greek subjects and territories under the Venetian control, this meant the changing of masters. In 1800, a number of islands in the Ionian Sea off the Adriatic were granted a Republic status under the suzerainty of Russia and the Sultan. France had briefly taken control with the fall of Venice. The main islands that came under this new entity include Corfu, Paxi, Lefkada, Cephalonia, Ithaca – the island that Homer mentioned in prose, Zakynthos, Kythera, which is actually in the Aegean off the Peloponnese."

"Some big words there Jack," said the Captain trying to understand what he was being told.

It was now the turn of the quieter Jimmy, after he too took a swig. The whiskey dripping down his long beard and dark olive features.

"Corfu, where I was born 50 years ago, is the most populous. The fort in the capital was one of the strongest in Europe circa 1799 when it was lost by the French to Russia. Greek and Italian languages are widely used. The region is overseen by Ioannis Kapodistrias; the foreign Minister of Russia oversaw governance. Lasting until 1807, the islands were ceded to France by Russia. This new arrangement was short lived. Seeing an opportunity to expand its Mediterranean influence, Britain took all of the islands using their dominant navy between 1809-1810. Now the British created a Federation which in many senses is a copy of America. Each island is to be treated as an individual state and they came together as a Federation. The President though, he is appointed by the Majesty, is an Englishman. After years of lawlessness in some of the areas, we need a Greek ruler not a foreign tyrant. Hence, our role in sabotaging anything British. We do not want them there."

The Captain had wished he hadn't asked.

The huddled group now fully understood why the men were risking their lives for people they barely knew.

———◆———

A not very sober Port Commissioner finally came out of his office, much to the relief of those on the water. The moment his thoroughbred was out of view, the crew made hasty preparations for a departure to the marshes via the Thames.

The river flowed all the way to London proper. From the outside, it seemed murky, filthy, untamed. Yet on the water, despite the narrow confines of the river, it was a breeze to sail on. The crew looked on in awe as warehouses, docksides, mansions, and markets clung to the edge of the water. Even with the fog, London looked impressive.

After two hours, the crew finally came to a halt just before the marshes at what appeared to be a quiet dock.

As soon as the anchor was laid and the boat tied, the crew was surrounded.

Alcibiades was the first to realise there was an issue. Had the Port Commissioner actually been competent? "Was he really going to see his mistress, and why would you give up your mistress to squeal on us?" He thought out aloud.

Byron smiled, as did Solon who recognised the insignia of their uniforms. Not very discreet to be fair.

Byron provided an update, "your friend Anamarci through her father was able to track down these fine old warriors. They are descendants of regiments that once protected the Emperor of the Greek Byzantines and some of their kind died fighting at Constantinople in 1453. This group of ten is all that remains of that bloodline and some of these men will hopefully meet me in Missolonghi in the not-too-distant future to fulfill their destiny. They are here for the honour of Greece. Some of their ancestors were with Emperor Manuel II Palaiologos on his visit to London in 1400, 1401, begging for the English to help against the Sultan. Our King Henry IV gave some money, about two thousand pounds, that was it. No men. No weapons. Today, they will help heal a wound that remains from that visit."

"They are also responsible for the transport," Pierre added. "These men are of Ukraine stock, living in Wales, though lately they have been perched at Rochester waiting for news of our arrival."

The Varangian Guard stood in military precision. There were no hugs or animated gestures. They took their inherited responsibilities seriously. As the full moon had risen to meet the faded sun, the Varangians marched in front, as silence descended upon the group. Not even a 'welcome to London, have a nice day' chat.

There was a small fleet of large wagons waiting. Lined up, one after the other. Pierre delegated each of the group to a Varangian driver. He provided them a map of different routes on how to get to the museum. Every member had a task for the moment they arrived.

Several of the Varangian were tasked to knock out the small group of guards, before the main gate and access to the side warehouse would be broken into. As the sale of the marbles had not been complete, it was likely that Melina's 'premonition' could be correct. A gamble. If they erred, they would fall back on plan Beta; take English artefacts to hold as a ransom swap deal!

21

A KNIGHT AT THE BRITISH MUSEUM

BYRON RODE WITH SOLON, MELINA and a ferocious looking Varangian who momentarily let his guard down.

"Sire, what do you know about the museum, I mean from when you visited? Does it compare to the great museums of Constantinople and Alexandria?"

He shook his well-groomed red hair as an answer for the latter question.

"My brave warrior, friend. Under King George, the British Museum Act came in 1753. And why?

All onboard the fast-moving carriage transport looked to Byron for the answer.

Byron became animated, "you see, a man from Ulster, Ireland, a doctor worked in London and built an extensive collection or art and other items. Perhaps 20,000 in total. He bequeathed this to the Crown."

"You mean an Irishman, enemies of England, helped precipitate this situation. Preposterous," Melina sounded angry.

Byron explained the situation further.

"I am sure he would have been as astounded as all of us over what happened in Athens and elsewhere, with Indigenous remains and artefacts and other territories losing prized possessions. Sadly, it has happened. The museum opened six years later in the mansion, Montagu House, Bloomsbury. In 1801, when Napoleon's General surrendered to the British, that surrender came with the Rosetta Stone. This is what is used to help interpret Egyptian hieroglyphs in the pyramids and tombs, giving us great power over Egypt, and great prestige in the world of arts and stolen artefacts. Since then, Roman collections have flourished and recently, the Bassae frieze taken from Phigaleia, have been added. There is a Building Committee drawing up plans to increase the size of the museum two folds. They need items to fill spaces and improve their prestige."

The passengers led by Melina were horrified, with the driver making just one point. "On behalf of all those unable to keep their treasures in their own lands, today we will strike back. The Greek world has consistently been pillaged since they lost Asia Minor. Enough."

———◆———

For each of the passengers, they marvelled at the site of the mansions, cobbled stone side streets, quaint buildings with chimneys. Chimneys were everywhere on all the roofs, a sure sign that Santa is welcome here. Alcibiades could not believe that such an amazing city could have a primitive urge to plunder foreign treasurers, not to mention the cruel barbarity of sending low level criminals to far away penal colonies. He had a certain pity in his heart for the rulers of such a beautiful land.

As each of the transports neared Russell Square, Solon, Alcibiades, Pierre and two Varangians hastily assembled as the first wave of intruder. Their task was simple, take out the troops assigned to protect the entrance.

Byron had explained that there would be just four. Two more would be posted in the grounds and two more inside. The mansion, once shut, is also able to shut out sounds from outside thanks to sturdy walls of stone.

Once inside the grounds, the warehouse doors would need to open to allow the transports in. From that point, it would become a game of hide and seek, to seek out the troops inside.

"I estimate we can take back the marbles within two hours and then we can head back in separate convoys again to the marshes." Byron had instructed everyone at the marshes.

The five men split into two groups, with the Varangians making the initial approach to the soldiers on guard duty.

The men nodded, assuming they were harmless passers-by. At the moment of passing by, the Varangian turned and delivered a flutter of punches to the two closest soldiers. The big black bearskin headgear proved a hindrance to the defenders and an easy target when being pummelled by a flurry of blows.

As quick as lighting, Pierre, Alcibiades, and Solon ganged up from behind to quickly subdue the remaining soldiers. A series of punches and kicks was enough to claim a quick victory, against the unsuspecting soldiers who would wake up with hangover-like symptoms. Though this hangover would be devoid of the fun drinking part, replaced by bruises and concussions. Solon began tying them up and gagging them to prevent any further noise.

Pierre took hold of a batch of keys, and on his first attempt, opened the door behind the soldiers.

A welcoming committee of two muskets awaited.

"Easy there gentlemen, we mean you no harm." Pierre explained, as blood from the last man he took out was undeniably on his black garment.

"Stop and turn around," one of the owners of the muskets with an itchy trigger finger shouted.

"Listen, by the time you shoot and reload, you both may kill or injure or even miss two of us." Pierre reasoned as the men fanned out. "Then, we will kill you. Or you can lay down your weapons and let us reclaim our artefacts and then we shall be gone. You will be lauded as heroes for preventing more theft and we will add you to our prayers as a thanks!" Solon reasoned.

The negotiation had no effect until a giant of a Varangian from the second contingent appeared, expertly throwing an axe which knocked both muskets from their masters. The two were easily overpowered and duly tied up. They too would feel the effects of a hangover minus the alcohol consumption. The soldiers were placed in a basement and locked there. In exchange for a guarantee not to hurt them further, they confessed that the pieces from Athens were being held in another basement. The keys to that entrance were on the two soldiers, patrolling inside the museum.

Another round of confrontation was brewing, this time led by Melina. By now, every member of the museum 'invasion' force was together. The Varangian guards were ready for action, Melina was a willing participant and Alcibiades had his rage to alleviate. The two former Ionian Islands natives were ready to take out their imprisonment under the British on these hapless Crown soldiers. When they found the two soldiers fast asleep, a nervous round of giggling broke out as they stared down at the two men almost huddling together. Would their wives approve?

The men woke and found muskets and xiphe swords pointing in their direction, as well as one angry Melina. Their surrender was easy enough with no hangover benefits. Tying them added to the collection of human prizes in the basement.

With all defenders now safely overpowered, the group went to work. With the tools at their disposal and the carry trolleys courtesy of the museum, one by one they were able to haul the prized possessions to the short distance of the transports. As each transport was loaded, it quietly departed from the main gate. Over the next two hours the stolen marbles were free.

Byron left a note:

"Thank you for keeping us in a cold climate, Really, we appreciate the hospitality. Now it is time for us to depart from this upstart location. Yours sincerely, the Greeks and a Knight at the British Museum. Post Scriptum, oh do please allow us to hear, some cheers, mighty cheers!"

The last convoy made it out with Jack and Jimmy and two of the Varangian Guards. Despite the chill of the night, they were sweating from nerves and adrenalin, just like the little monster would daily.

"We are the rear, we must get back to the vessel, unload quickly and get out to the Channel. The tide and wind will be in our favour, though every minute will count now. And I hate counting!" It was Jack speaking to the prized possessions. "Do not worry, you are free now."

The horses picked up apace, which aroused the suspicion of patrolling Police Officer Bobby. He caught a glimpse of the dark olive-skinned Greek men and one giant Varangian and he blew his whistle. Several other uniformed police officers answered the call. They had been inspecting a local brothel and were due back to their station.

Jack now pressed the horses harder. "We have been made, hurry."

Now the heat and the chase was on.

The thoroughbreds of the police were gaining ground. The giant Varangian jumped onto the roof of the transport as one rider sidled up close. He used what appeared to be his python muscles to smash him in his helmet, laughing as he watched him fall off his white horse. The next rider too came close and politely asked the transport to pull over.

"Allo sir, could you kindly halt please and we can talk about this over tea."

He too met a similar fate as the Varangian did not drink tea.

With several hundred feet to the vessel, with its ramp waiting for the last cases of precious cargo, the people on the boat looked on.

Jack and Jimmy knew what had to be done. Their fate had perhaps always been a trip to Botany Bay or Van Diemen's Land.

"Our giant friend, we will jump off and deal with the police. Try to pile as many cases as you can into your pythons and just abandon the rest. Get the boat sailing, do not wait for us."

The giant nodded and readied himself for what came next. The two Greeks jumped at the four riders who quickly started a fist fight. The giant stopped the transport at the narrow ramp, taking as many cases as he could carry.

"Sail. SAIL, do not wait, goooooooo," he barked loud enough for residents as far as Gipsy Hill, the second highest point of London, to hear.

The captain and crew were ready to sail and needed no further incentive as more police arrived on the scene. The ropes holding the boat to land was untied and the vessel pushed off.

22

AN UNEXPECTED DEPARTURE

AT THIS TIME OF THE night, police could only follow them along the Thames, though within an hour they would be back in a larger body of water and then to the open sea. Without a means to communicate to the Royal Navy, the freed marbles were as good as rescued. Nonetheless, two riders shadowed the vessel in the hope that it would be caught in shallow water or a change in the wind. The riders would be heroes and possibly promoted to such roles as Port Commissioner. Their hope was forlorn once the 'assailants' had passed the small working-class port of Tilbury and Ciffe pools on the other side. Once the latter was rounded, the body of water opened significantly.

The Captain had ensured a British flag flew to avoid arousing any suspicion, now prepared to replace the Union Jack with the flag of France.

Meanwhile, the two Greek men who remained behind, were bloodied, bruised and content, finally surrendered to the large mob of police who had surrounded and fought them with batons and a cat o' nine tails. Just like the priceless cargo that was rescued, they too would end up on a ship leaving the Thames. For a different destination.

—•—

Dawn began to escape from its night-time imprisonment, something the marbles achieved with a little help. The adrenaline of all onboard ensured that nobody slept, and no-one wore a coat. Land was starting to disappear behind them. A welcoming France would be there for them in several days as they would have to negotiate the high wind and a sea that refused to calm down, slowing them significantly.

"Great, we rescue the marbles and then we sink to the bottom of the ocean!" Eleftheria mused.

"It is ok my cousin; these things happen. Just means we will have to go slower and longer until we reach the safety of France. Besides, if we sink, I am positive we can find some divers from Kalymnos to retrieve the rescued crates."

"And who will dive to retrieve us Alcibiades?"

"Good point," he laughed at Eleftheria. I think it is an opportune time to pray anyway, and afterwards we need to sleep. Nothing more we can do.

———◆———

The sun had risen early, birds circled and chirped, and the sea was calmer and fresh. The calm before another storm as the overladen ship approached the French coast. Finally, the mission would be complete. No more drama or stress for the group.

The Captain came to the deck and summoned the group to him. "Come on everyone, come up." He was ringing a bell to attain attention.

He held a musket. In his belt he had a six-shooter revolver.

"Team, it has been wonderful working together. It has been an experience and one that I will tell my grandkids someday…."

Bang. It was Alcibiades from behind. Aside from always running or jogging on Greek time, he had been delayed by the call of nature and was last on deck. The Captain had failed to notice an absent Alcibiades. It was evident that the Captain now sought to steal the priceless treasures of cargo. Though judging by the pleas of his crew, it was a solo job. Melina took possession of the weapons.

"Go on, get up there, walk that creaking plank….."

The captain reluctantly did as he was bade. He walked briskly as he knew his fate.

"You can dive, or you can be shot. Either way, my suggestion is that you swim with the current towards old blighty," she said, pointing the American six shooter gun.

"Think of it this way old chap, you will make history as the first ever person to swim the Channel if you succeed. Maybe one day they will have a Channel swimming race in your honour! Unlike you, we are not bandits. We will leave the vessel and crew, should they wish to wait for you, at Calais. Should you ever make it back!"

Pierre shed a tear. He gave the Captain a kiss on both cheeks. "I can't say I am not disappointed. A leader should have honour." He then shoved the dishonoured Captain hard, hard enough that Alcibiades had to grab him to keep him from falling as well.

The entire crew stood at the bow and waved. A loud cheer went up.

"First mate, please set a course to the second pier of Calais, where another surprise awaits," Byron said as enthusiastically as he could.

Byron knew that news of the heist would make its way over to Calais, and it would be a clever idea for all and sundry to vanish into the breeze of the continent.

As the vessel made its way into the welcoming harbour, a woman could be seen on the dock, an elegant woman.

"Alcibiades, we know of her." It was Solon's turn to be enthusiastic.

"Yes, my friends, Laskarina Bouboulina was told of a possible heist from France. At first, we all expected it to be in Paris, not in London. Obviously, this changed somewhat. Next up, when Pierre left us for two days, he also found the time to get a message to Bouboulina who was in Marseilles to come meet us for a possible package. As you can see, she did not bring just one ship. She has brought an escort in case there are more greedy serpents in the water like the one swimming the Channel now.

The elegant woman and the pier came closer to view. Much to the relief of everyone on deck.

23

AEGEAN SEVEN

Disembarkation came swiftly, for Bouboulina was in a hurry to return home. The spirit of revolution was brewing, and she had plans to contribute. The Ottomans had recently attempted to take some of her ships; her tenacity and fierceness along with the manding sword she kept with her, was enough to help her hold on to her ships. It was rumoured her sword was dripping with poison.

The Varangian Guard, after helping transfer the precious cargo, marched in unison. The boarded the main ship, which was decked with cannons and Greek would-be independence soldiers from Spetses and the Morea.

"Where will our treasurers end up?" Solon enquired of Bouboulina and Byron.

"Ioannis Kapodistrias, the Russian Foreign Minister and co-founder of "Philomuse Society" which promotes Philhellenism, has arranged a fortified safe haven on the island of Hydra. The island is well fortified and is poised to play a significant role when the uprising eventually begins." Byron answered.

"How many of you fine heroes, the *Aegean Seven*, will board my ship as my guest?" Bouboulina enquired.

"Aegean Seven?" asked Melina.

"Yes, you lot and a special woman in Athens have been whispered as such in the Greek world, a nice title that befits you all."

Everyone in the Aegean Seven smiled. Exhausted.

"I need to return to Calabria, home. I can go wherever that enables me to return to my town, husband and people." It was Eleftheria, half pleading.

"Bova Marina is a friendly Greko town. I will be glad to stop by to restock and recoup for a night." Bouboulina offered.

Alcibiades confided, "I will be making my way to Odessa. Therefore, Hydra is fine, and from there I will make a special visit to my home, Athens, and to locate the beautiful 'owner' of the Milano scented perfume, which seems popular in Athens. Well, with one amazing goddess of Athens, anyway!"

Melina offered on behalf of Solon, "we will take the opportunity to ride through the continent again with a stopover in Venice. Byron has invited us to stay a few days to relax and enjoy. We can catch up with his assistant Rooney. We may visit Ravenna and then eventually settle in at Thessaloniki. By that time, it will be time to start a family." She looked gazingly at her partner. Without breaking her stare, "we need more Greeks, more of us, not less."

It was the turn of the Frenchman, "well, for me, I will come part of the way as I will join you and Byron for a short holiday at Geneva. After that, it is back to the Mediterranean for me. I have seen enough war, hatred, and anger to last me ten lifetimes. I intend to organise a Greek Liberty Committee in the old Greek colonies, and we can help from afar for when the time arises. Zhto H Ellas, Freedom for Greece." Contributed Pierre.

Zhto H Ellas, Freedom for Greece. The group chanted over and over as tears flowed. Something remarkable had been achieved, yet this was only just the beginning for the Aegean Seven.

A burst wind eased past the talkative Aegean Seven. It's other member, Alcibiades looked at the distance with a sense of pride, a pride that was matched by his beating heart and Hellenic blue blood coursing through his veins.

Alcibiades would soon utter an oath before a Priest in Athens as part of his initiation to the next adventure he was about to embark on. Tattooed across his mind were the immortal words:

*I swear in the name of truth and justice, before the Supreme Being, to guard, by sacrificing my own life, and suffering the hardest toils, the mystery, which shall be explained to me and that I shall respond with the truth whatever I am asked. ***

By the time Alcibiades arrived by boat to Odessa in 1817, there was no turning back the colossal tide of freedom. It would be the start of a freedom that was originally denied the stolen marbles, Zhto H Ellas.

*Sacred Oath taken by members of Filiki Eteria

The End, for now

Image 1 British Museum, 'Acropolis Collection' credit Bruce Whittingham

Image 2 Cathedral of Elgin, credit Marco Sardi

Image 3 Lord Byron, credit Georgios Kollidas

Image 4 British Museum, 'Acropolis Collection' credit Bruce Whittingham

Image 5 Parthenon, credit Scaliger

Image 6 Four Bronze Statues, credit Meinzahn

Image 7 British Museum, 'Acropolis Collection' credit Bruce Whittingham

Image 8 Laskarina Bouboulina, credit Georgios Kollidas

Image 9 Headquarters of the Filiki Eteria, Odessa credit Billy Cotsis

Image 10 British Museum, 'Acropolis Collection' credit Bruce Whittingham

All photos from Dreamstime, except 8

Two Greko sayings used in this book are from the Costa Vertzayias book, The Greek Speaking Communities of Southern Italy. Please find ways to support the Greko of Calabria and the Griko of Apulia. You may seek out the documentaries below or reach out to these communities. Just like the Acropolis, these people are a link to an ancient Greek past, a glorious period for the Hellenes.

ABOUT THE AUTHOR
OF THE NOVEL

Billy Cotsis was born in Sydney to parents from the island of Lesvos, in 1977. He spent almost a year of his childhood in Greece.

Upon entering university in 1995, he joined the well-organised and active Greek club, Macquarie University Greek Association. He spent four years learning more about and promoting his own culture before making his way to Greece, again, in 1999. The love affair with Greece was rekindled. From that time onward he has spent most of his spare time researching his own Greek roots from Asia Minor and Lesvos as well as becoming fascinated with the remnants of Greek settlements in countries outside of Greece.

At last count, he had made his way to almost 60 countries and 79 Greek nisia. A prolific writer, with over 350 of his articles appearing in Greek media in various countries.

Since 2012, he has written 17 short film and documentary projects, contributes to a blog

https://herculean.wordpress.com/ which features all of his history articles and has written or been involved with six book titles.

An avid Manchester United and Canterbury Bulldogs fan, Billy is currently working on a feature film called, Once upon a time in Crystal Palace.

BOOK TITLES

Aegean Seven 2022

1453: Constantinople & the Immortal Rulers or there are no dogs here 2020

Once upon a time in Crystal Palace, Heart, football and life under Brexit: a fiction told by a Greek Aussie 2019

Fairwater Foodies Cookbook, Frasers Property Australia, editor/coordinator, contributor 2018

From Pyrrhus to Cyprus Forgotten and Remembered Hellenic Kingdoms, Territories, Entities & a Fiefdom 2017

The Many Faces of Hellenic Culture 2016

*Most of these can be found on Amazon or the Greek Bilingual Bookshop

Filmography

40 Hellenes in 40 Cities 2022

Magna Graecia: a visit to the Greko of Reggio 2021

Fabio's Tale of Olives 2020

Magna Graecia: the Greko of Calabria 2020

GRASSROOTS 2019

Magna Graecia: the Griko of Apulia 2019

An Olive Tale I&II: a journey through Italy and Greece 2019*

An Olive Tale in Apulia short film 2018

Mykonos: the other side 2018

Bromance: Zorba gets a Girlfriend 2016

Lesvos: fall in Love 2015

The Draconian Decision of the German Drachma 1 2015

The Draconian Decision of the German Drachma 2 2014

Brutus vs Caesar: Winner takes London 2014

Leadership 2014
Zorba goes to Sydney 2013
*A Sandhurst Fine Foods Australia project
YouTube Channel: Billy Wood https://www.youtube.com/
    channel/UCOduNv0Uh2iLMUEkof89oMg

Made in United States
North Haven, CT
04 December 2024

61581635R00090